ALIEN IMPACT

ALIEN IMPACT

E. C. TUBB

WILDSIDE PRESS

INTRODUCTION

BY PHILIP HARBOTTLE

British science fiction author Edwin Charles Tubb died in his sleep at his London home on Friday, 10th September, 2010. He was born in London on October 19, 1919, and married Iris Kathleen Smith in 1944. He is survived by their two daughters, Jennifer and Linda, granddaughters Lisa John and Julie Hickmott, and several great grandchildren.

Writing as E. C. Tubb, he became particularly well known to readers of science fiction the world over, his work having been translated into more than a dozen languages. Beginning in 1951, he published over 130 novels, and more than 230 short stories in such magazines as *Astounding/Analog, Authentic, Galaxy, Nebula, New Worlds, Science Fantasy, Vision of Tomorrow*, and in more recent years in *Fantasy Adventures,* published by Borgo/Wildside. Many of his short stories were reprinted in various "World's Best SF" anthologies, and his 1970 *Vision of Tomorrow* short story "Lucifer" won the Europa Prize in 1972. It was later much anthologized, most notably in *Flight or Fright,* edited by Stephen King and Bev Vincent, and is currently in production as a film.

Tubb was appointed editor of *Authentic Science Fiction in* 1956, and edited it with great panache until its unnecessary demise in 1957.

His writing ambitions had been born shortly before the Second World War, when he became a fan of the American science fiction pulp magazines then being imported into Britain. In his early teens, he became an avid collector, and began to make contact with fellow enthusiasts, eventually joining the pre-war

British Science Fiction Association in his native London. The outbreak of the war put paid to his early writing ambitions, but after the war, the members of the old Science Fiction Association—who included Tubb's fellow enthusiasts Frank Arnold, Ken Chapman, John Carnell, Walter Gillings and authors John Beynon Harris (John Wyndham), Sydney J. Bounds, Arthur C. Clarke, and William F. Temple—began to reform. Tubb became a regular attendee at their meetings, and this group of fans and fledgling professionals eventually launched their own sf magazines, *New Worlds* and *Science Fantasy*, to which Tubb became a regular contributor. Within a year of his debut as a short story writer, Tubb began producing novels.

His early books were exciting adventure stories, written in the prevailing fashion of the early 1950s, which demanded that stories should be fast moving, and above all else, entertaining. Yet from his very first 1951 novel, *Saturn Patrol* aka *The Warbirds* (Wildside, 2021) Tubb's work was characterized at all times by a sense of plausibility, logic, and human insight.

These qualities were even more evident in his short stories, which tended to a more thoughtful, psychological type of story, so that by 1956 Tubb's short stories began to be reprinted in Judith Merril's prestigious *Year's Best Science Fiction* series of anthologies. Many of his short stories continued to be reprinted in various later "World's Best SF" anthologies. His haunting short story"Little Girl Lost" (1955) was adapted for American television for Rod Serling's prestigious *Night Gallery* series in 1972. In 1988, his novelette "Kalgan the Golden" (1955) was adapted as a graphic novel by Philip Harbottle and artist Ron Turner.

Tubb's first major SF novels were *Alien Dust* (1955) a gritty story of Martian colonization, and *The Space Born* (1956), a highly original take on the "generation Starship" theme, that anticipated by decades the central theme of *Logan's Run*. In 1962, *The Space Born* was adapted as a 90-minute television play by Radio Television Francaise.

When the British market for SF novels slumped after 1954, Tubb diversified into writing pseudonymous paperback Western novels. Many of them were based on actual historic events during and after the Civil War, and were considered notable enough to earn the author an entry in *Twentieth Century Western Writers* (St. James, 1991) and to be reprinted fifty years later in both hardcover and paperback, where they are still in print. Tubb later became very interested in Roman history, and many consider that some of his best written work was contained in his trilogy, *Atilus The Slave* (1975), *Atilus the Gladiator* (1975), and *Atilus the Lanista* (first published as part of *Gladiator,*1978). All three novels are exclusively still available in Wildside editions.

Because many of his numerous SF short stories of the 1950s and early 1960s were under pseudonyms they tended to be overlooked at the time, so that despite continued commercial success, Tubb never received the critical recognition he deserved. Many of his ideas were seminal, and were later reused by other writers to popular acclaim—most notably his short story "Precedent" (1952) positing the grim and logical solution to the problem of stowaways in spaceships, appearing more than two years before Tom Godwin's more famous "The Cold Equations." But eventually Tubb became renowned in America—and the rest of the world—for his long-running "Dumarest of Terra" series of novels, beginning with *The Winds of Gath* in 1967. The galaxy-spanning saga of Earl Dumarest and his search to find his way back across the stars to the legendary lost planet where he was born—Earth. Its worldwide commercial success caused Tubb to more or less abandon the short story form. Dumarest is currently under option for a television series, and the books are currently available as Audio Books, and E-Books.

Following the death of American editor and publisher Don Wollheim—who had first commissioned the series—the Dumarest saga came to a premature end after 31 novels, with

The Temple of Truth (1985) However, the 32nd novel, *The Return*, had already been written, but at first was only published in a French translation. Its first English publication was by Gryphon Books, a New York Small Press, in 1997. The series seemed to have ended on an inconclusive note, and it was not until Tubb, at the age of 90, wrote a final novel at the urging of his agent, that the saga was brought to a conclusion with *Child of Earth* (Homeworld Press, 2009).

The Tall Adventurer, a comprehensive, worldwide annotated bibliography, compiled by Philip Harbottle and Sean Wallace, was published by Beccon Publications in 1998. This sparked a further wave of reprints by several publishers in the US and the UK, and throughout Europe in translation. Further European critical recognition came in July 2010, when *I Posseduti,* the Italian translation of his novel *The Possessed* (1959, revised 2005) won the Premio Italia Award, being voted best International Novel.

New collections of Tubb's short stories continue to appear worldwide, following the success of Wildside's *The Best Science Fiction of E.C. Tubb* (2003, and still in print in both hardcover and paperback). Definitive French language collections, *Dimension: E.C. Tubb* edited by Richard D. Nolane have been published by Riviere Blanche since 2012.

* * * *

Despite failing health in later years, he continued to both revise old books and short stories, and to produce new novels. A major dystopian novel *To Dream Again* was accepted on the same day as the author died, and was published by Ulverscroft in 2011. His final, and possibly his most outstanding novel, *Fires of Satan* was published posthumously in 2013. Amongst his other later titles, of especial note were *Footsteps of Angels* (2004), *Dead Weight* (2007), and *Starslave* (2010).

All of these novels are included in Wildside's ambitious rediscovery series of new reprints, bringing Tubb's work to the attention of modern readers!

CHAPTER ONE

MEETING AT MIDNIGHT

The tall man had white skin, white hair, red eyes. He said: "Mr. Warren?"

Jim Warren tried to peer past his midnight visitor. Beyond the tall man, fog swirled, making the starless night even blacker than normal. He stared at the Venusian.

"What do you want?"

"May I enter?"

"I suppose so," Jim stood aside, letting the man pass him, then slammed shut the rough timber door. He stood, back pressed against the panel, watching.

The Venusian smiled thinly, glanced once about the mean room, seated himself at the rickety table.

"Won't you join me?" He spoke Terran without a trace of accent. Jim flushed at the condescending tone, dropped into the remaining chair.

"This isn't a social visit," he snapped. "For the second time, what do you want?"

"Later," the Venusian gestured vaguely. "It is the custom to offer refreshments to the visiting guest," he reminded.

"On Venus," Jim agreed. "I am a Terran."

"We are on Venus," smiled the man. "And I am a native."

Jim hesitated, then reaching within a locker produced a squat bottle and a couple of chipped glasses. He slammed them down upon the table. "My apologies," he said. "I have no reason to love your race."

"Nor your own either?"

"That's my affair."

"It could be mine, Mr. Warren."

Jim poured a thick green wine from the bottle, filling the glasses to the brim. He emptied his own at a swallow, refilled it.

"You do not drink?"

"No."

"I didn't get your name. What is it?"

"I didn't give it," answered the tall native calmly. "You may refer to me as Fleetan."

"Fleetan," murmured Jim. "Fleetan? Where have I heard that name before?"

"I have no idea." The visitor delicately touched the chipped glass. "Perhaps it would be as well if you didn't strain your memory. Some things are best forgotten," he laughed. "As you say on Earth, 'let sleeping dogs lie'."

"Is that what you came to tell me?"

"No. I do not pay midnight visits to hovels on the edge of the settlement to exchange old sayings."

"What is it then?" Jim snapped impatiently. "Get to the point, or get out."

Fleetan inhaled sharply, the breath hissing between pointed teeth. A tinge of colour wavered in the alabaster whiteness of his cheeks.

"It is not wise to use such language to one of the pure blood," he warned. "I am not one of your whining half-breeds, neither Terran or Venusian. They are worthy only of contempt. A curse upon them!"

Jim shrugged. "The night grows old," he said soothingly. "You must be weary. It is not good for a host to weary his guest. Wine?"

Fleetan looked his pleasure at the ceremonial form of language. He glanced shrewdly at the Earthman.

"You have the ancient usages of speech. Strange in one of your world. Do you speak Venusian?"

"A word or two, no more," lied Jim. "Once it interested me. Now…" he shrugged, gesturing towards the ruinous hovel of his living quarters.

"I understand," Fleetan nodded. "It was touching upon this matter that I came. Tell me, would you accept employment?"

"Would I what?" Jim stared at his guest. "Of course I would, you know that, everyone knows it, but what's the use? They all know me. Jim Warren, renegade, sot, coward." His voice held bitterness. "Spare your anger, I know what they call me. I'm a useless failure. I can thank you and yours for it."

"Can you?" Fleetan's voice held contempt. "You were an idealist. A man who was going to right a great wrong. You were going to prove that Terrans and Venusians were related, that we had sprung from the same racial stock." His hand clenched around the glass. "Did you ever pause to think that we didn't want your proof? Did you really believe that we would be proud of such a relationship?"

"Why not? Do you always want to be regarded as alien?"

"Are we? Is it not rather you who are alien? We are a proud race, our records trace our descent from gods who arrived on wings of flame. Twenty thousand of your years ago. Tell me, for how long do the records of Earth extend?"

"Does it matter?" Jim asked dully. "What else could your gods be than men. Men arriving on wings of flame. Tell me Fleetan, have you never seen a rocket ship? Isn't that what you would call wings of flame?"

"Blasphemous dog!" The Venusian sprang to his feet, one slender hand darting to within the robe of fine spun silk he wore. Jim grinned at him without humour.

"Going to kill me, Fleetan? Is that your way of conversion? Why not just deride me? Deny me access to your secret records. Complain about me to the Terran authorities. Accuse me of peddling drugs, agitating the half-breeds to revolt. You did it before. Why not do it again?"

"It isn't necessary," Fleetan smiled with thin colourless lips. "You are a broken man. No one in authority would listen to you, no matter what you had to tell them. That is why you can be of service to us."

"Service to you," Jim laughed. "Now I know that you are mad."

"Am I? Tell me Warren, would you like to return home?"

"Home!" Jim breathed. "Earth! The Sun and Moon again instead of eternal clouds. Fresh clean air, instead of the spore laden muck. To see real men and women. To feel the wind, swim in the sea. Home! You may hate me, Fleetan, but I didn't know your race was sadistic."

"You misjudge us, Warren. I offer you a chance of returning to your planet. There is one condition."

"Yes?"

"You do as I say, implicitly, without question. You must remember that your loyalties are with me, and act accordingly."

Jim frowned. "You are asking a lot. What do you want me to do?"

Fleetan toyed with the glass of heavy green wine. He appeared to be listening, his free hand hidden by a fold of his robe.

"What is it?" Jim snapped suspiciously.

"I may have been followed here," admitted the Venusian calmly. "My attendants should have scoured the area by now, and reported to me. They are late."

"Who would want to listen to our conversation? I haven't spoken to Veni or Terran for months. Why should they follow you?"

"That is my affair. You are merely an instrument that may be of value to me. Obey, and ask no questions."

"Now get this, Fleetan. I may be ostracised by every Earth-man on this hell planet. I may be cursed by them, denied passage home, an outcast from my own people, but I'm still a

Terran, and I'll do what I want to do, when I want to it." He rose, strode to the door. "Now get out!"

"What! You dare?" Fleetan sprang to his feet in a smooth ripple of effortless motion, his eyes blazing red. "Scum! Dog of a Terran! Filth!"

Jim smiled, walked stiff-legged towards the snarling native. He clenched big hands, his dark eyes mirroring hate. Desperately the Venusian tugged at what was hidden beneath his robe. Metal shone dully in the weak light thrown by the primitive lamp, swung, centred on the menacing Terran.

"Back!" snarled Fleetan. "Back or I'll shoot!"

"Go ahead," invited Jim. "What have I got to live for?"

Suddenly he lunged, twisting his body to one side. The weapon whispered, the Venusian swinging the slender barrel to bear upon the elusive form of the Terran. He screamed as he felt hard hands grip him, the weapon dropping from nerveless fingers. Deliberately Jim drove his fist into the delicate features.

"Fool!" he spat. "As I thought, a needle gun." Carefully he picked the tiny darts from the thick leather of his jacket. "Did you forget I'm not one of your naked savages?" He laughed as he picked up the weapon. "A toy. Deadly against bare skin or thinly clad flesh, but you forgot that, didn't you Fleetan? You forgot that all Terrans wear clothes!"

Cautiously he collected the venom-tipped darts, ground them into the soft loam with his boot heel. The weapon he slipped into a pocket. Deliberately he advanced towards the prostrate native.

"Get up."

Fleetan scrambled to his feet, his red eyes glaring murderous rage. "What do you intend?"

"Intend? Nothing. You came here with a proposition. I am interested in it. Continue."

Fleetan stared at him, rubbing the darkening spot where he had been struck. His flickering eyes alighted on the untouched glass of wine. Greedily he drank it.

"I fail to understand," he said, "I tried to kill you."

Jim gestured the objection aside. "I told you that I am a Terran, Fleetan. We are a logical race. We have found over the course of time that it does not pay to harbour grudges. You tried to kill me, yes. I stopped you with a blow. We are both alive. I suggest that we get down to the business on hand." He squinted at the native. "Or are your personal feelings of greater importance?"

"I see; a strange race," Fleetan shook his head and sat down. "I must give you formal warning," he said stiffly. "I have been insulted, you have laid violent hands on one of the Elder Race. For that you must die. Of that there can be no question."

"Do you kill me now, or after I have finished the job?"

"Do not mock," rapped Fleetan sharply. "You know enough of our customs to know that I speak of what must be."

"I understand," Jim said quietly. "Between us this debt of blood must be washed away. I know your custom, and I respect it." He smiled. "Strange when you come to think of it. If I had shot at you, tried to poison you, done anything but actually laid hands on you, this situation would never have arisen. Tell me, Fleetan. Why do your people have such an exaggerated respect for personal privacy?"

"It was so in the beginning," Fleetan answered sonorously.

"And what was good enough for your father is good enough for you," Jim shrugged. "Well now that we know how we stand, how about getting on with it?"

"The position is this," Fleetan said, pouring more wine. "Ridiculous as it may be, some of your wild reports have aroused interest on your home planet. A small group has been appointed to make an official investigation. They should arrive very soon."

"You mean an actual Government investigation?" Jim slammed his fist onto the table. "At last!"

"No," corrected the Venusian. "Not a Government investigation, a private one. It appears that there are certain small groups who have long harboured your same theory of mutual origins. They have subscribed, and are sending a small group to investigate first hand. Naturally they will receive the minimum of official assistance, we have seen to that."

"Naturally," said Jim dryly. "Where do I come in?"

"On arrival they will seek you out. You will meet them, act as their guide, disillusion them, and send them home convinced that your entire theory is merely a product of a wild imagination."

"But why me?"

"Because you are the one most likely to convince them. You are the one whose reports have excited them, the one held to be an authority on the subject. Your final rebuttal of your own theory will convince them as nothing else would."

"And if I agree to do all this?"

"I am empowered to offer you a sum of currency, sufficient to enable you to purchase a passage to your home planet."

"I see." Jim sat deep in thought for a while. "How are you going to convince the port authorities that I should be granted clearance papers? You know my position."

"That will present no difficulty. The port officer will be persuaded that your presence on Venus constitutes a threat to the common welfare. It would be unpleasant if a Terran should be found murdered."

"How are you going to kill me?"

Fleetan smiled thinly. "Have no fear. The affair will be conducted with due regard to the customs. Well?"

"Do I agree you mean?" Jim slowly poured wine. "I think that it could be arranged. I shall need access to the records of course, unhindered travel facilities, all the help possible to obtain. I think that I would be willing to help you on those terms."

"Are you insane?" Fleetan stiffened in his seat. "You ask the impossible, the Watchers would never allow it."

"They'd better," retorted Jim grimly. "You don't understand the Terran mentality, I do. The harder a thing is to get, the more valuable it becomes. If you try to hide anything, you will only draw attention to it. Allow the party to examine the records; they won't be able to decipher them, so what harm could it do?"

"Could you decipher them, Warren?"

Jim gestured impatiently. "You know I couldn't. I asked for your help before; you refused it, how do you expect me to be able to read a language that I can't even speak?"

"Maybe you are correct, you should know the workings of the minds of your own people better than I." Fleetan frowned at the dirty table. "I cannot promise, it does not rest with me to decide, but will you do as asked?"

"On one condition."

"Yes?"

"You do not offer me enough. I want treble the sum mentioned."

Fleetan hesitated for a moment. "Granted."

"It is well," Jim said ceremoniously. "Will the guest take wine before his departure?"

"The host is gracious," retorted Fleetan. "A little perhaps. The weapon?"

"A memento of a notable visit," replied Jim smoothly. "To be cherished for a while, then returned at the next meeting."

Fleetan rose, gathered his silken robe about him, stepped to one side as Jim moved to unbar the door.

"A pleasant journey," he murmured, holding the rough panel open.

Fleetan stared at him for a moment, then uttered a stream of Venusian. With an effort Jim kept the blank look he wore.

"My thanks for your greeting," he said. "Goodnight." He locked the door behind the tall figure of the native.

He spat, trying to rid his memory of the stream of insulting filth the Venusian had spat at him in parting. He tapped his pockets, gingerly removed the captured weapon, and laid it carefully on the table.

From the locker he took a pipe, its bowl carved in strange configurations. Stuffing it with fragrant weed, he lit it at the naked wick of the primitive lamp. Seating himself at the table, he poured wine, slowly drank it.

The room grew heavy with smoke, the weapon glittered dully before him on the table; the level of the wine in the squat bottle shrank. From time to time he smiled.

It was late when he blew out the lamp.

CHAPTER TWO

PHEELAN

Ben Pheelan owned a dive on the edge of the landing field, a low wooden hut selling cheap food and cheaper drinks. He was one of the growing number of half-breeds, a man who'd had a Venusian mother and a Terran father. The inevitable result was that he was wanted by neither race, and despised by both.

A thick-set man, reaching middle age, with the white skin of his mother, and the black hair, blue eyes, and irascible temper of his father. He leaned across the stained counter, glowering at a solitary man seated at one of the corner tables.

A short man, like the majority of space travellers. A dark-haired, brown-eyed man. A man who stared at the high wire fence separating the landing field and environs from the native quarter. A man who smoked a pipe the bowl of which was carved in curious configurations. A Terran.

Pheelan wiped the rough wood of the counter, hitched at his belt, and strode with quiet menace towards the lone figure.

"I've been watching you," he growled. "You've bought one drink, and nursed it for the past two hours. This place isn't a rest room. Drink up, and get out."

Jim looked up at the sturdy figure of the proprietor. Deliberately he took the pipe from between his lips, finished his drink.

"You've changed your tune, Pheelan. Once you told me that I would always be welcome here."

The big half-breed stared, his eyes narrowing, then he grinned, stuck out a huge paw. "Jim! Jim Warren! I haven't seen you since your trouble started. Where have you been?"

"Around," Jim answered laconically. "How are things with you, Ben?"

"Not so good." Pheelan slumped into a vacant seat, snapped impatient fingers at a young girl. "Bring wine, the best," he frowned down at the stained table, fingers idly caressing a savagely scarred cheek. "Things are getting worse, Jim. I'm under orders to quit. The Venusian Council have passed a law restricting ownership of property, or continuance of trade to native born only," he grinned savagely. "Do I have to explain that native born means pure blooded?"

"No. How about the port officer? Will he consider leasing a concession within the area?"

"Not a hope. I've seen him, begged with him, he was quite nice about it, but only Terrestrials need apply," Pheelan glowered. "What do they want, Jim? Is it our fault that we were born? We're human, just the same as any Terran, as any Veni for that matter, but neither of them want us. Can you understand it?"

"I think so. It isn't a new thing, Ben. We've had something like this on Earth for thousands of years. A despised race, an unwanted race. It took a long time for nations to become tolerant towards them. They did no harm, but they had a few racial characteristics, a different form of worship. They were harmless, law abiding, pleasant enough people, but they suffered for a long time."

"How long do you think we're going to suffer, Jim?" Pheelan asked grimly. "The new generations are growing up, and we number several hundred. It would take a little to arouse them, set off something to bring our plight to the notice of the Terran authorities. We could do it, Jim."

"Revolt you mean?" Warren shook his head. "The wrong way, Pheelan. You would be wiped out."

"Would we?" the dive owner smiled suggestively.

"Maybe not. We wouldn't attack with bare hands or primitive weapons, we're not savages. Supposing that several hundred men were armed with Wilson guns? How long do you think that the settlement would last? Why, we could form a new government, rule Venus as it should be ruled. It would be the best thing that could happen for both our worlds."

"Wilson guns?" Warren looked grim. "You try that, Pheelan, and you'll know what atomics are like. The Terran authorities would blast half the planet to dust in retaliation if you tried anything like that. Anyway, where would you get Wilson guns from?"

Pheelan shrugged, turned as the young girl brought the wine. He watched her as she set the bottle down, his eyes followed her as she swung lithely away.

"Your daughter?" Jim asked.

"Yes. Her mother and I are both half-breed. What do you think of her?"

"A beautiful girl," Jim said cautiously. "On Earth she would be considered truly lovely."

"On Earth perhaps," Pheelan sighed, poured wine. "Yet how is she ever going to get to Earth? You know the emigration laws. None but Terrans or true-blooded Venusians. For some reason they are afraid of us. Why, Jim? Why?"

Warren sighed, toying with his glass of glistening green wine. "An old ruling, Ben. Like all things it was meant for the best. It was done to prevent the introduction of possibly harmful elements to Earth's economy. A few mutated fungi spores, for example, would devastate the tropic zone. Natural, uncrossed types, would not be able to survive, they would find the environment too alien to support them. It was never meant to apply to humans."

"Then why do they enforce it?"

"Because it's in the rule book, until the old law is changed, it must still be enforced. I'd hoped to change it. I failed."

"I know, Jim. We had high hopes of your researches."

Jim shrugged, changed the subject. "Tell me, Pheelan, do you know of a man named Fleetan? A tall man. A member of the Elder Race, whatever that is?"

"Fleetan? I think I do. A proud man. Wears a silken robe with the insignia of the Anero Tanap?"

"Anero Tanap—the hidden place," Jim nodded. "That would be the man."

"A dreamer. An idealist. A man hungry for power." Pheelan looked sharply at the Terran. "What do you know of him?"

"Little," admitted Jim. "I heard his name, saw him once, wondered about him. Is he to be trusted?"

"Is anyone?" the big half-breed asked cynically. "Where his own ends are to be served, he is to be relied on, but he shifts with the wind. He will use a man, then cast him aside. He has great influence with the Watchers, is high in the inner-most circle of the Council, has access to the port authorities. He has been to Earth, studied in one of your Universities. A proud man."

"Would he be a man able to obtain Wilson guns?" Warren asked softly.

Pheelan started, the scar on his cheek standing lurid against the whiteness. "Some things are best forgotten," he grated.

Jim bowed his head a little, his pipe sending a great cloud of fragrant smoke coiling towards the low roof.

"It is forgotten," he promised quietly.

Something darkened the door. Three men, trimly clad in the blue and silver of the Terran space fleet, crowded through the narrow opening. Jim slunk back into the shadows as he saw them, the big proprietor bowing, wiping his hands against the side of his trousers, as he advanced to serve them.

"Your pleasure, sirs?"

"Wine, you old villain," yelled the leader of the trio. "Wine, green as jealous sin. Wine to wash away the taste of space flight. Wine to welcome members of your new garrison."

Phlegmatically, Pheelan set bottles and glasses before the men. He had seen their type before, new arrivals to the permanent garrison, out on a spree. Their heads were full of tall stories, their egos inflated with self-importance. Harmless enough usually, but sometimes ugly rumours followed them back to Earth.

They poured the glasses full, gulped the potent wine, refilled the glasses. Elbows on the counter, they arrogantly surveyed the low-ceilinged room.

"Bring on the girls," yelled one of them, a red-haired youngster. "I've money to burn, and I want company."

"There are no women here, sir," Pheelan explained quietly. "They are all in the settlement, it is rare that we see one in the native quarter."

"Rare?" The youth looked his amazement, then roared with laughter. "Why you old fool, I don't mean Earth women. They are within the fence yonder. Prim little misses. Nurses, clerks, wives of the port officers. I want to meet some real women, who would be proud to associate with a man of Earth."

"We have no such here," replied Pheelan curtly.

"No? Then who was your mother? You're no native born. Where there's one there will be others."

"We have no such," repeated Pheelan stubbornly. He flexed the great muscles of his hands. "My mother was a good woman; she died when I was born. I must ask you to keep a guard on your tongue."

"I apologise," the youth said indifferently. "But listen, you are a man of the world, you know what I want. Here," he poured a glittering stream of coins from one hand to the other. "I am not mean. Surely you know of some lonely little lady who would be eager to be kind to a rich young space man?"

"I must ask you to leave," Pheelan snorted, the scar on his cheek mottled and red.

"When I'm ready," said the youth carelessly. "What do you see, Frank?"

The leader of the trio chuckled, and pointed to the curtain back of the bar. "A pretty lass, the best on Venus I'd say. Fetch her out bartender, ask her to share wine with us."

"My daughter drinks with no man."

"What? And you a seller of wine," the leader shook his head in mock reproach. "That is no way to get rich. Tell me, wouldn't you like to see your daughter accepted by Terrans?"

"No." There was an insult in the way the single word was spoken. The spacemen caught it, flushed with sudden, anger.

"What do you mean, half-breed?"

"I mean this," said Pheelan quietly. "If you are representative of your race, then the sooner you leave Venus the better. As for my daughter drinking with scum like you, I'd sooner see her dead at my feet. Do I make myself plain?"

"Yes," the tall Terran breathed deeply, little spots of colour wavering in his cheeks. "Very plain. Listen you dog of a half-breed. Venusians are low, but what could be lower than such as you. Animal. Stand aside, I'll show you what I think of your precious daughter."

"Get out," said Pheelan quietly.

"Try and put me out," invited the spaceman sneeringly. He took a deliberate stride forward. The smack of flesh against flesh sounded strangely loud.

Pheelan stood above the unconscious form of the arrogant spaceman, fist still clenched, a thin line of blood crossing his knuckles where they had split against the fallen man's teeth. He breathed deeply, a dazed look in his eyes. Warren rose quietly to his feet, the wine bottle swinging from one hand.

The red-headed youth stared down at his fallen leader with shocked amazement, amazement which quickly turned into murderous rage.

"You swine!" he spat. "To strike an Earthman. Get him, Tony." Together they began to sidle towards the proprietor.

"Hold it!"

At the sound of a strange voice, they jerked around, tensed. The red-headed youth squinted at the approaching figure of Warren.

"Better get out of here, you've broken the regulations. If you don't want to be confined to barracks, keep this quiet."

"Who are you?"

"Never mind who I am," Jim said easily. He held the bottle hidden against the side of his leg. "I'm a Terran if you must know, and I saw everything that happened. Your friend asked for all he got, and you know it. Now pick him up, get him to bed, and we'll forget the whole thing."

"Will we?" questioned the red-headed youth softly. His hand fumbled at the back of his belt. "I think I know you. Warren, isn't it? I've heard of you, Warren."

"Have you? Something nice I hope?"

"Very nice," the man sucked in his breath with a faint slobbering sound. "Outlawed aren't you? Beyond Earth's protection. Despised even lower than the half-breeds. Yes, I've heard of you, Warren."

He began to chuckle to himself. The hand behind his back slowly came into view. He held something, something which clicked sharply; suddenly his hand spouted a length of glittering steel.

The bottle smashed full into the sneering features.

Jim stared down at the bleeding unconscious figure, the rumpled uniform stained and dirty. He wiped his face, and grinned at the trembling figure of the proprietor.

"Good work, Ben," he gestured towards the slumped body of the third man. "What did you hit him with?"

"My hand—he's not hurt much, but I couldn't take chances. What shall we do, Jim?"

Warren shrugged. "What can we do?"

Pheelan began to sweat. "You know what this means, Jim. When they report that they were beaten up in my place, I'll be thrown in jail. I'll get ten years!"

"No you won't," Jim calmed. "Listen. They won't talk, if they do, then they will have to say what they were doing in the native quarter. Terran jurisdiction does not extend beyond the barrier, that is why I'm still free. You think that the port authorities wouldn't like to deport me?" he smiled thinly.

"But what about them? They can't stop here."

"I know that. Let me think." Warren stood moment looking down at the unconscious figures. "We'd better drag them outside; when they recover they can make their own way back. In the meantime, you'd better pack your gear, get out while you can."

Pheelan grunted. "I thought you said they couldn't report me?"

"They won't, but they have friends. How would like the whole garrison to come in here, and wreck place?" Jim grinned savagely. "How did you get t scar, Pheelan?"

"In a brawl," absently answered the half-breed. He looked up in sudden concern. "My daughter!"

"Now you know why you had better leave. Sell out, go into hiding for a while. I'll try to calm things down."

"You?" Despite himself Pheelan smiled. "What could you do? A man more despised than I am."

"I am a Terran," said Jim. "I have certain rights."

The big proprietor didn't answer.

Together they examined the contents of the three men's pockets. Jim grunted as he saw the amount of currency they had; enviously he fingered it. "They deserve to be robbed," he snapped.

"Well?" Pheelan looked questioningly at the pale Earthman.

"I'm not yet that low," Jim snapped angrily. He picked up the red-headed man's weapon. "A folding knife," he murmured. "Spring-loaded blade. A nice toy." He folded the blade, sprung it open a few times.

"I'll keep this. I want something for my trouble. Anyway, it's illegal for him to have it," he dropped the knife into a pocket.

Thunder blasted through the humid air. A siren wailed from the watch tower on the edge of the field. Jim jerked upright, letting the unconscious man slump to the floor.

"The space ship. Pheelan, I must go. Can you manage without me?"

"I can get help," grunted the big proprietor. "When shall I meet you again?"

"I'll contact you. In the meanwhile keep out of sight, and Pheelan," he stared at the big man. "Don't do anything rash. You know what I mean."

"Yes. I know what you mean," the big man nodded slowly. "But, Jim, something had better happen soon."

Warren nodded, ran from the dive. Above, in the cloud-wreathed heavens, fire blazed from the thundering venturis of a descending space ship. The roar of its passage dinned in his ears, the flare from the multiple tubes almost blinded him.

He was running by the time he reached the gate.

CHAPTER THREE

AT THE HOUSE OF WELCOME

He needn't have hurried. Thrusting his way through the jostling bunch of natives and half-breeds, Warren panted up to the closed wire gate of the settlement.

"Warren," he gasped to the scowling guard. "Has the Port Commander sent down a pass for me?"

"Warren? No."

"Are you sure?" Jim pleaded.

"Certain," grunted the guard. "You can enter if you like," he invited hopefully. "I'm sure that the Commander would be pleased to see you."

"I don't doubt it," replied Jim dryly. He turned away. The scene beyond the twenty foot wire fence held little to interest him. The towering shape of the space vessel, now discharging cargo and passengers, the ring of warehouses and living quarters, the low huts of the garrison, all were familiar, he had seen them before.

A tall Venusian bumped into him, whispered in his ear.

"From Fleetan. The House of Welcome, in an hour." Jim tried to locate who had whispered the message, but he was lost in the crowd, shrugging, the Terran weaved his way towards the heart of the native quarter.

The House of Welcome was a pitiful attempt by the Venusians to ape the customs of Earth. There were no hotels on Venus. Hospitality was demanded as a right, and no home, however poor, would dream of either refusing it, or of asking payment. This had worked successfully for a while after the impact of Earthmen, then there had been ugly rumours. Men had been found lying in the gutters, dead. Venusians had complained that their guests had behaved like wild animals once freed of the iron discipline of the garrison. As a compromise, the House of Welcome had been hastily erected.

Jim swung through the crowd, making an unerring way to where the slender tower of the hotel peeped over the low roofs of the surrounding village.

A Venusian hissed welcome at him as he entered. He stood, blank-faced, while the native translated.

"Your pleasure, sir?"

"My name is Warren. You have a reservation for me." He uttered the flat statement in a coldly unemotional tone.

"Yes, sir. Will you retire to your room?"

"Yes."

He followed the native through a winding corridor, up two flights of stairs, and into a pleasant enough room. It had wide windows, opening onto an unspoiled garden. The lush growth of ferns, vines, great blossoms of variated hues, filled the air with delicate perfume, the faint drone of insect wings threw a soft murmur from the shielding walls.

The click of the door made him turn. Fleetan stood just within the room.

"You are quick," said Jim. "I have only just arrived."

"I know," said the Venusian tersely. "I was informed." He still wore the soft robe with the sacred symbol, in addition he had a thin fillet of gold about his temples, and from one finger blazed the fire of a giant ruby. A dark bruise showed against one cheek, he touched it gently.

"Admiring your handiwork, Warren?"

"What is happening?" Jim snapped, ignoring the remark. "I understood that I was to receive a pass enabling me to meet the new arrivals on the field. There was no pass. Did the party arrive?"

"They did."

"Then why wasn't I permitted to greet them?"

"That has been taken care of. You will enter the picture later, after they have settled the details of arrival. They will reside here."

"Why? Why not in the settlement?"

"Why should they?" Fleetan arched thin brows. "After all, they have come a long way just to study us. How can they do that within the settlement?"

Jim grunted, slumped into a chair, ran a dry tongue over parched lips.

"Wine?" Fleetan touched a thin cord. To the native who entered, he spat a stream of Venusian, the man bowed, left, returned with a great beaker of emerald wine. Gratefully Jim poured out a generous measure.

"When will the party get here? How many are there? What equipment are they bringing?"

"They will arrive soon, there are three of them, a woman and two men. They have no equipment."

"Damn!" Jim jerked upright in the soft bottomed chair. "You say they have no equipment? No cameras? No recorders? What kind of an expedition do they call themselves?" He gulped wine.

"It was not intended that they should bring the means of recording things better not seen by irreverent eyes," Fleetan said coldly. "They will observe, take notes, listen to you, to the local authority, and they will leave, disappointed no doubt, but convinced that you are mistaken."

"And I leave with them," said Jim. He held out his hand. "Where's my money?"

"You will get paid when the job is done," Fleetan answered coldly.

Jim reared to his feet, his eyes had a glazed look. "I want my money, you double-crosser. Give me the money, or I don't play," he swayed drunkenly, flopped back into the chair.

Fleetan smiled at him grimly.

"You will receive what is due to you," he assured softly. "In the meanwhile, more wine?"

"Thanks," Jim tilted the glass, let green liquor rill down his chin. "You're a good fellow, Veni. I love you. I love you all," he collapsed in drunken laughter.

The door swung quietly open.

They were dressed, the three of them, in the regulation Terrans' attire. Drill shirt and trousers, tucked into the tops of high boots of soft leather. A short leather jacket completed their attire. The first to enter, smiled at Fleetan, held out his hand.

"Mr. Fleetan?" My name is Jack Conroy, this is Professor Masters, and this is his daughter Daphne." The Venusian bowed, ignoring the proffered hand. Conroy flushed, looked foolish, and abruptly dropped the hand.

Jim giggled.

"Mustn't be annoyed old man," Warren slurred. "Venusians don't like being touched, not those of the Elder Race anyway, and they don't use a prefix. Just Fleetan. He won't mind, will you, Veni?"

Fleetan smiled thinly, gestured apologetically towards Warren. "Please don't take offence. Our ways are not the ways of Earth. As Mr. Warren explained somewhat incoherently, we do not permit personal physical contact, also we do not have a prefix to our names, nor do we use more than one. I'm sure that you will understand that no insult was intended."

Conroy smiled, his thin upper lip with its trace of moustache curling as he did so.

"Who is the drunk?" he asked, jerking a finger towards Warren.

"That? That is Mr. Warren, an authority on the subject that interests you. I personally feel that he is mistaken. I make no secret of that fact, but nothing would delight me more than to find that there is some grain of truth in his theory, however wild it may appear. Unfortunately, Mr. Warren has suffered some reverses in his quest. He has, however, found some degree of comfort in our local wine." Fleetan looked significantly at the great container of liquid. Conroy sniggered understandingly.

Professor Masters grunted, looked his disgust. "Did he know that we were coming?"

"I informed him myself," replied the Venusian, smoothly.

Jim struggled to his feet. His head spun with the effects of the drugged wine and he cursed himself for drinking it. Not that he'd had any choice; to keep in character, he dare not admit any knowledge of the Venusian tongue; to have refused the wine would have made Fleetan suspicious. He clutched at his stomach.

"Excuse me," he hiccupped. "Don't go away, back soon." He reeled out of the room. Ten minutes later he returned, red-eyed, trembling, shivering with cold sweats. The antidote he had swallowed burned his stomach, but he was sober. He smiled weakly as he entered the room.

"I believe that we've already been introduced," he said. "I don't remember it too well, but I'll pick up your names as we go along."

"I am glad that you feel better, Mr. Warren," Fleetan said stiffly. "I will leave you to talk things over between yourselves."

"Why not stay, Fleetan?" Jack Conroy urged. "I feel that you could be of great assistance to us."

"I wish that I could, but the rules of my order," he glanced at the glowing ring on his finger, "demand my presence elsewhere. However, feel free to call on me at any time." He bowed himself from the room. An uncomfortable silence descended.

"Did you bring any recording instruments?" Jim snapped curtly.

"Unfortunately, no." Professor Masters rubbed his short beard. "We intended to, of course, but somehow they were left behind. I hope to be able to borrow something from the port officials."

"I doubt if that will be possible," snapped Jim. "It was an unpardonable oversight. I trust that you will not make such errors in the future."

"I hardly think that you are justified in throwing recriminations," dryly protested Masters. "Your condition on our arrival did not engender confidence."

"I was drunk," admitted Jim. "Now I'm sober. What are your plans?"

"We intend either to prove or disprove your contention that Earth and Venus are inhabited by a common race. I was relying on you to guide our investigations."

"Good." Jim sat down, reached a hand out to the container of wine, frowned and drew it back. "To commence with, the colouring of the natives is exactly what one would expect if Earthmen were subject to the same climate. They are not exactly albinos; yet the continual absence of direct sunlight has brought them to within the verge of that state. They are as nearly devoid of protective pigment as is possible without actually being albino."

Masters nodded, checking the points on the fingers of one hand.

"Physically, they are identical to Earthmen. They are alien to their environment; by that I mean that the flora and fauna are not compatible to a mammalian race. Venus is still, geologically speaking, in the Mesozoic period. The fauna is comprised of Dinosaurs, the flora of giant fungi and ferns. There should, logically, be no mammalian life."

"Correct," agreed Masters.

"The final, and to my mind, the most conclusive of all reasons is a simple biological one. The two races are able to breed together. The proof is all around us."

"A good point," said Masters. "A very good point, but not conclusive. What else is there?"

"What more do you need?" snapped Jim, irritably. The fumes of the wine made his head ache. "There are legends, of course. Their records speak of gods arriving on wings of flame some twenty thousand years ago. They have secret records, records which, I feel sure, would prove it one way or another. They have a mysterious priesthood, the Watchers. There is a hidden place, the Anero Tanap, which is sacred, a sort of holy land. To me there is no doubt."

"I must study them," declared Masters. "I will lodge here and study them."

"If you do that, then you will be wasting your time," Jim reached for his pipe, lit it and puffed fragrant smoke. "You will not find the true culture here. This place is a cancer, polluted by Terrans and Terrestrial ideas. This hotel is one. No. The true Venusian is to be found far in the jungles. There are clearings, there are villages; there is a system of communication, unbelievably efficient. This place is a sort of trash heap."

"But Fleetan, the others, what of them?"

"Fleetan is a renegade to his own people; at least that is what some natives think of him."

"Do you?" Masters asked shrewdly.

"Me? What I think doesn't matter, but think for a moment. Fleetan is high in the inner circle of the Secret Council. He is favoured by the Watchers. I wouldn't be surprised to find that he is more than what he seems; the rest of the natives who hang around the port you can discount."

"You mean that they are similar to the coloured people back home; at least, similar to what they used to be?" Daphne leaned forward intently. "When a member of a primitive tribe learned European culture he was no longer a member of a primitive tribe. Whatever he was, better or worse, he was no longer representative."

"Correct," Jim agreed. "You have a neat way of putting it. The only thing worth studying here is the half breeds. This is the only place on Venus that you will find them."

"Why is that?" asked Conroy.

"Because they are the tragedy of the whole affair. Think of it. They are not allowed to travel to Earth. They are not allowed within the settlement. They are not allowed to own property or to conduct trade. They are the great unwanted. Despised by both races, owned by none."

"And so they cling to the settlement?"

"They are not allowed to leave the settlement," corrected Jim grimly. "The Watchers see to that."

"You have mentioned the Watchers several times," Masters said. "Just what are they?"

Jim grinned tightly. "They watch," he said. "Just that."

"But…?"

"Leave it at that; I don't want to talk about it at present," his voice was very sharp. He reached again towards the wine, remembered the drug and silently cursed.

"Notice the colour of the wine?" he asked, hopefully.

"Yes, an odd colour," Daphne mused interestedly. "What causes it?"

"The natives brew it from a species of fungi; it is surprisingly potent and comparatively cheap. They have another kind of wine, a yellow one. I think that you would a like it. Shall I order some?" He reached for the bell cord.

"I don't think so…" began Masters, but the entrance of a native cut his words short.

"Wine," ordered Jim. "Yellow wine for the guests." He lifted the glass, still full of the green liquid. The native bowed, returned with a slender bottle full of thick, yellow wine. Eagerly Jim tilted the bottle.

"Here," he offered glasses around. "Let's drink to the success of your venture." He gulped greedily at the glass refilled it. The others had not touched their drinks.

"What's the matter? The wine is harmless."

Daphne set down her glass, smiled understandingly at him. "You know, Mr. Warren," she said gently, "you don't have to have an excuse to drink. We understand."

"Thank you for nothing," he said bitterly. "Do you think I'm a sot? All the rest do. A drunken fool with his head in the clouds." Savagely he drained his glass.

"I'm sorry," apologised Daphne. "To our venture!" She sipped at the thick, yellow fluid, made a surprised face, drank it down. "Why, it's perfect!"

"If you drank that on Earth it would cost you a hundred credits a bottle," Jim told them bitterly.

Masters drank, looked hard at Conroy. The blond effete-looking man sipped delicately; swallowed obviously; smiled weakly. "Good stuff!" he said. "I'll bet the first explorers thought the journey worthwhile just to get a bottle." He winked.

Jim stared down at his glass, the thick, hand-manufactured article held little glimmers of trapped light. The knuckles whitened, the tendons standing out with sudden strain. Abruptly the glass smashed in his grip. A trickle of blood rolled from his palm to the leaf-covered floor.

"You've hurt yourself!" cried Daphne. She advanced, a tiny square of linen in one hand.

"Forget it!" snapped Jim savagely. "There's no harm done. I can always drink from the bottle."

He stumbled from the room.

CHAPTER FOUR

THE STORM

Jim awoke with a throbbing head, and a tongue coated with what seemed to be fur. He squinted his eyes against the glare of late morning, stared at several empty bottles, groaned, sat upright on the low bed.

He staggered a little on his way to the shower, flinched beneath the icy stream of water, then dressed with shaking hands. He was lighting his pipe when the knock came the door.

"Come in!"

Daphne entered, trimly dressed, fresh-faced, her skin still faintly tanned from the sunlight of Earth. She smiled.

"Hello! How are you feeling now?"

"Fine. Why shouldn't I be?"

"You seemed to be ill last night. How is your hand?"

"That?" Jim shrugged. "A scratch: think nothing of it. Had breakfast?"

"Hours ago." She hesitated, looking at him with her wide eyes holding an unspoken question.

"You are wondering if I drink like this all the time," Jim said flatly. "I'll save you the bother of asking. I don't."

"I'm glad of that," she said simply.

"Don't be. I don't drink because I can't afford to. Now you know. Well?"

She smiled. "You know, I don't really believe that you are as bad as you try to make people think."

"Thank you." Jim didn't smile. "What are the others do-ing?"

"Jack and my father have gone with Fleetan to see the port officials. They are going to bring our things here. I want to look over the settlement."

"Good idea."

"I thought that perhaps you would be willing to act as guide?"

Jim thought for a moment, then shrugged. "Why not?"

"Good. Shall we go, then, or would you rather eat first?"

"I've eaten," Jim said curtly. He led the way from the room.

Outside the thick humidity of the Venusian day swirled about them. The sun, a great patch of golden light, rode high in the heavens. Jim sniffed at the air, squinted at the surging mass of clouds, tested the fitful wind.

"What's the matter?"

"Nothing."

"Nothing?"

"There may be a storm," snapped Jim irritably. "It won't be serious." He led the way through the thronging crowd of natives, half-breeds and the occasional Terran. A seller of native art called to them as they passed his booth.

"Step this way, visitors from the stars. Step this way and examine these wondrous works of Venus. None better are to be found. Cheap."

Jim frowned distastefully as the wheedling tones fell on his ears. He lengthened his stride. Daphne tugged at his sleeve.

"What is it?"

"Can't we look at his things?"

"If you want to," snapped Jim. "But don't let him know that you like them. If you want anything, let me do the haggling."

They stepped to the little counter laden with the merchant's stock of worked leather, jewelled ornaments, weapons, tiny flasks of oil, dwarf plants, beaten metal and all the other trappings of the merchant's trade. He rubbed his hands as they stopped, began a persuasive discourse on the merits of his stock.

"A jewelled ring for the lady? A wallet of finest nagar hide for the gentleman? Souvenirs of your sojourn Venus. All cheap."

"Save your breath, fruit for the Watchers," Jim snarled. "I am no Terran tourist."

The man took a sharp breath, his hand automatically flickering to the odd-shaped scar on his forehead. "What do you know of the Watchers?"

"They watch," Jim answered with grim humour, turned to Daphne. "Do you care for any of these things?"

"What is this?" she asked, touching a delicately fashioned and jewelled instrument of wood and metal.

"A weapon. An ingenious thing. It shoots a cloud of parasitic spores; the results are very unpleasant and quite lethal. It isn't loaded, of course."

"And this?"

Jim looked at the tiny vial of murky, yellow flecked glass. Within, something golden moved in slow, hypnotic convulsions. He smiled, held it in his hand. The golden glow changed to a rippling tide of ever-changing colour beneath the warmth of his hand.

"A toy, the Venusians make them for the children play with," he gestured towards the merchant. "How much for this?"

"That, sir? That very rare object of our ancient science? I would not dream of parting with it for less than one hundred interplanetary credits."

Jim tossed it back onto the counter. "Five."

"But, sir, consider, where on Earth would you find such an object? For seventy it would be a bargain."

Jim turned to Daphne. "Lend me five credits." He tossed the note towards the merchant. "Satisfied?"

"Impossible!" The man gestured wildly. "You insult my wares to offer such a sum. Fifty now would be nearer the worth of the exquisite article."

"You wear a strange scar for a man of Venus," Jim murmured. "What penalties do the Watchers demand for any who betray the pride of their race?"

The man began to sweat. "I accept your offer," he hissed, then in forlorn hope. "Perhaps the Earth girl cares for my wares?"

Daphne bought a similar toy, a curiously carved ring, and a wallet of the fantastically soft leather. Jim flung notes on the counter, spun her away from the scowling merchant.

"Let's get out of here," he growled. "These people make me sick."

"But why, Jim? Surely they have a right to earn a living?"

"Like this?" he gestured around the edges of the high wire fence. "The half-breeds do it because they can do nothing else. The pure-blooded Venusians, however…" he spat in disgust.

She shrugged her arm away from his grip. "I don't understand you," she said coldly. "You profess to want to help these people, yet all I have heard you do is insult them."

"You haven't seen what I have," Jim looked around, spotted the low door of a wine shop, led her within the dim interior.

The proprietor, a half-breed with red hair, bowed before them.

"Your pleasure, sir?"

"Wine, the best you have," Jim ordered. He sat at one of the little tables. Daphne hesitated for a moment, then sat beside him.

"What's the matter, Jim? Why are you so bitter?"

He didn't answer. The tavern keeper brought wine in a thick glass open-necked jug. Jim poured the green liquid into two long stemmed goblets, drank deeply. "I've seen history made," he said quietly, staring into the depths of the wine. "And I don't like what I see."

"Tell me," Daphne persuaded gently. She lifted the goblet to her lips.

"When the first ship from Earth landed, they found a natural people, proud, simple-living, sane. For a while the two races respected each other; the men of Venus could acknowledge the daring of the men of Earth, the restless courage which drove them to journey to the stars, even though they could not understand it. The Earthmen found in the simple, proud culture of the Venusians something to be wondered at. Mutual respect kept the two races on a friendly footing. Now?"

"Aren't things just the same?"

"Are they? Would you think so, after seeing those peddling touts? If you were the average visitor to Venus, what would you think?"

Daphne hesitated, toying with her glass. "I see what you mean," she admitted.

"Tourists never see Venus, not the real Venus. What they see is a tiny patch of artificial culture, nurtured and bred by themselves alone. When the first expedition landed almost forty years ago, insanity was unknown here. Venusians just did not suffer from mental aberration, neurosis, psychological disturbances. Within the past ten years insanity has risen from one percent, to well over fifteen. Is it any wonder that this whole area is under quarantine?"

"Quarantine?"

"Yes. Few people, even Terrans, know it, but this entire area for a distance of twenty miles each way from the landing field, is quarantined. The natives know it, the half-breeds, a few port officials, but the news is kept from the visitors."

"But why, Jim? Why are we quarantined?"

"Because we carry the seeds of a terrible malady. For some reason Venusians cannot ape our ways. If they try it they go insane. The impact of our culture on that of Venus is mental death to them. They know it."

"But why should they, Jim? Why couldn't they just keep on with their own ways?"

"Do you remember reading the history of the North American Indians? The Aztecs? The Chinese? What happened to them? They didn't ask for the foreign invasions: they wanted to be left alone. When invasion swept them aside, what happened to them? They lost their pride, they lost the power of being themselves. They aped their conquerors and lost their self-respect. The Venusians don't want to follow the same path."

"Aren't you exaggerating things a little, Jim? After all, we only want to help them. With what we can do for them, help them to build roads, develop their planet, surely they should be grateful to us."

"Are you making the same mistake as those back home?" Jim asked bitterly. "Hasn't it occurred to you that this is their planet? Has it never struck you that perhaps we have more to learn than they have? Roads, mines, shipping lines—are they really necessary to a contented life?" He swirled the wine in his goblet.

"Perhaps not," agreed the girl. "But at least we are trying to do good. Can we be blamed for that?"

Thunder rumbled in the far distance; the light grew dim; a hint of menace seemed to fill the thick, humid air. The sounds of men shouting came clearly to their ears. Merchants busied themselves piling their goods within leather covers, others ran along the narrow streets bearing great bundles on their backs.

"The storm," explained Jim to the girl's enquiring stare. "It will be upon us soon."

"Will it be very bad?"

"Not very." He reached for the jug of wine. "There's nothing we can do until it breaks and the rains have had time to wash away. The jungle will be impassable for a while." He poured the goblets full. "Tell me, did you notice anything while you were in the market? About the natives, I mean?"

"I don't know." She frowned, trying to think of what he meant. "They all spoke Terran, is that it?"

"In a way; but did you notice that they all spoke in the same way? Half-breeds, Terrans, natives all spoke Terran with the same inflection, the same accent, or rather lack of it."

"Now you mention it, they did. Why is that?"

"No Terran has ever learned Venusian, a few words, perhaps, but not the full language. It is one of their most closely guarded secrets. If any Venusian were to be caught teaching a Terran his native tongue, he would die horribly." Jim smiled grimly. "That is a proven fact."

"Why is that, Jim?"

He shrugged. "Who knows? The result, of course, is that all Venusians coming into contact with Earthmen speak Terran. The half-breeds can speak nothing else. It has had an interesting result."

"How do you mean?"

"As all the crews of the early ships were of a reasonably high level of culture, the language they taught was also of a high standard. So we get natives and half-breeds speaking the same as cultured Terrans. We also get everyone speaking almost exactly the same. No idiom, no class slang, no excuse for not understanding each other perfectly."

"Isn't that rather a good thing?"

"Is it? How can we ever learn about them when we cannot even guess at how their minds work? A natural language is a product of the way a race thinks. For argument's sake, supposing the Venusians used emotional ideas instead of strict definition, as we do; wouldn't the change from their natural way of communication lead to mental upset? Incidentally, it is only the natives who suffer from insanity, not the half-breeds, who have spoken nothing but Terran from the day of their birth."

"That brings up a question, something that has been troubling me." Daphne hesitated, biting her lip. "What happens to the mothers of these children? The mothers of Terran-fathered children, I mean."

Jim stared at his glass in sudden bitterness. "They die," he said curtly. "Sometimes in childbirth, mostly by other means. Not all of them, of course; the Venusians are not a cruel people, but few of the women accept the alternative."

"What is that?"

"To have the child taken from them at birth. Never to see the infant again; to be banished from all contact with Terrans."

"How cruel!"

"No," said Jim quietly. "You see the Venusians are a very moral race. They realise that human nature is weak; they do not condemn the woman for associating with an Earthman, marrying him, bearing his child; but they insist that the infant must not weaken the pure strain. The woman is offered the alternative—lose the child or death. The child is never harmed."

"Is there no way out?"

"So far," Jim said bitterly, "no Terran has ever taken his wife and child back to Earth with him."

"Couldn't they stay within the settlement?"

"Not while the laws are as they are." Jim fumbled for his pipe, trying to master the rage he always felt when he thought of the self-satisfied Terrans, safe behind their wire fence. They were hard laws, unfair laws; the Terrans admitted it themselves, but they were also convenient laws.

A few drops of rain spattered the soft loam of the ground, sending up a fine spray of mist. A faint drumming began to echo from the low roof. The air, already chokingly humid, became difficult to breathe.

"You have a strange name," Jim said abruptly. "Daphne. An old-fashioned name. I thought that girls called themselves Sellene, or Titania, even Luna, nowadays."

"I had old-fashioned parents," she explained. "It was my mother's name. After she died I didn't like to change it. Father seems to get comfort from calling me the same name as mother had."

Jim nodded, sending great streamers of smoke coiling upwards from the odd-shaped pipe. The storm had come, the rain drumming on the roof with a sound that made conversation difficult. Outside, the street had turned into a lane of liquid mud, the fierce torrent lashing the soft loam into a glutinous mess.

The proprietor leaned against the counter, idly watching the two sole inmates of his tavern. He rubbed a vague hand through his mass of red hair. The faint tan on Daphne's skin seemed to fascinate him. He jerked suddenly alert as someone almost fell through the low doorway. A man, mud-spattered, gasping for breath, his thick chest heaving, staggered into the tavern. He stood for a moment adjusting his eyes to the gloom, then half stumbled towards the only occupied table.

Jim sprang to his feet as the man advanced, gripped a white, mud-coated shoulder. "What is it?"

"Quick!" gasped Pheelan. "Come quick! They are out of my control!"

Jim nodded, followed the man out of the dive. It wasn't until after that he realised they had spoken in Venusian.

CHAPTER FIVE

THE INSURRECTIONISTS

The rain hammered at him, smashing down on his unprotected head, drenching him to the skin. The ground mist made things difficult to see. Twice he almost fell, slipping in the ankle-deep mud. He yelled for his guide to halt.

"Where are we going?"

Pheelan looked blank.

Jim tried again. "Where are you taking me?" he yelled at the top of his voice. Seeing the questioning look flung at him, he shrugged, gripped Pheelan's belt and plunged through the mud after his guide.

They hadn't far to travel. A few short lanes, growing narrower and meaner as they progressed, and Pheelan stopped before the low door of a tavern. He ducked inside, Jim at his heels. Within, they wiped their eyes, cleared their ears, grimaced at each other.

"What's the matter?" Jim snapped.

"I had to get you, Jim," Pheelan apologised. "I can't do anything with them. They've nursed their grievances too long, and Jim, I feel that something's wrong somewhere."

Jim squinted around the few idle natives in the single room of the wine shop. "Where are they?"

Pheelan hesitated.

"If you want me to do anything, I'll have to see them," Jim said impatiently. "Where are they?"

"In the old warehouse of Sam Glaath," Pheelan admitted. "They began to assemble just before the rains. I tried to reason with them, but they won't listen. They laughed at me; called me a coward. Someone's agitating them, Jim. I'm afraid that there will be trouble, big trouble. You've got to stop them."

"I see." Jim looked sharply at the half-breed. "Are they armed?"

"Yes," admitted the big man.

"Wilson guns?"

Pheelan nodded. Jim cursed savagely.

"Take me to them, Pheelan. The blind, stupid fools Do they want to throw everything I've been working for into the gutter?" He slammed a fist into his palm. "Take me to them."

Once again they plunged into the rain. Diving down twisting lanes, slipping on the edges of rain-filled hole which would have swallowed them without trace. A building loomed through the mist, a decrepit old construction of wood lashed with rusty wire. Pheelan kicked at the low sagging door, snarled impatiently as a shutter slid aside.

"Pheelan and Warren. Let us in."

The door swung protestingly open.

A young man stood by the door. He had a peculiar dark skin and black, crinkled hair. He looked sulkily at them. A long barrelled Wilson gun rested against the edge of the frame. Jim snatched it up as he passed.

"Where are the others?"

The young man made a grab at his weapon, then nursed his arm as Jim smashed it savagely aside with the long barrel.

"I said, where are the others?"

"In the rear of the building," the man muttered.

"Lead us! I said *lead us.*" Jim swung the Wilson gun, prodding the doorkeeper in the stomach. "Move!"

Reluctantly the young man led the way into the depths of the building. Jim stood just within the rotting doorway, the Wilson gun swinging from one hand, surveying the scene before him.

About a hundred men were gathered into the dim ware-house. All of them were young, all bore the unmistakable stamp of dual parentage. All were armed with Wilson guns.

Boxes of ammunition stood open on the floor, their contents of copper charges for guns gleaming dully in the gloom. Several containers of wine stood next to them, many empty, a few spilt; the heavy odour of the liquid tainting the thick air.

Gradually silence descended as the excited youths grew aware of Warren's presence. Several of them looked abashed, half-heartedly trying to hide their guns. The majority stared at him boldly, fingering their weapons.

"Don't point those guns at me," Jim rapped sharply. He stared at them with cold eyes. "Do any of you know what you're supposed to be doing?"

A burly, thick-set young man strode to the front of the crowd. "We're doing what we should have done years ago; what should have been done when the Earthmen first landed. We're going to wipe them out."

"Are you?" Jim asked coldly. "And when more ships come, what then?"

"We'll kill them, too."

"And when an army arrives?"

"We'll kill them all as they land. It won't last long. When they realise that we don't want them there'll be no more ships." A murmur from the crowd told of their agreement with the speaker.

"What fools you are!" Jim sneered his contempt at them. "You hope to stop a world by killing a few individuals. Let me tell you nothing will ever stop Terrans from coming here. Nothing. Do you understand?" He let his eyes flicker over the crowd.

"I know Earthmen. I am one. I know how they respond to a challenge. You can kill the garrison. You can kill a million of them as they land, one after the other; you can kill until your weapons wear to dust in your hands and still they will come.

Never underrate the power of Earth, they are at their best when it comes to war."

"Talk," sneered the burly young man. "Terran talk."

"Is it?" Jim smiled grimly. "What do you know of war? Have you ever experienced it? In one war alone, a war between two of the great nations, tribes if you like, ten million men died. Ten million! Can you realise the number? Of course you can't, but if each of you killed every man assembled here, he would have to do it one hundred-thousand times. It would be impossible to do it; you would die of old age before the thing was done—and you talk of war." Again his eyes flickered over the crowd.

"What of it?" insisted the man uneasily. "They haven't the men here; it takes time for the ships to arrive."

"Agreed. But do you know what will happen? I do. They will arrive and you will kill them. They will send more men, and more, and still you will kill them. Then they will send ships loaded with radidust. They will spray it over the area and every single living thing will die. The trees, the fungi, the insects, the animals, the worms in the soil—and the men on it. All will die. They will wait five years, maybe ten, and when they return there will be no eyes to see them."

He straightened against the doorway on which he had been leaning. "Why are you here? Who talked you into this rash action? Answer me! Who agitated you?"

Several of the crowd looked towards a yellow-haired man at the rear of the hall. He tried to hide, then stood boldly alone, as if by accident his Wilson gun swung towards the door.

"I may have said something," he admitted. "But I wasn't the only one."

"Who filled your head with this nonsense?" Jim demanded. "Who talked you into this mad plan? What was it you were to do?"

"One of us was each to mark a Terran. At a signal we were to strike. Then onto the settlement, where some of us would already have killed the garrison, wrecked the radio and taken over the quarters." The burly young man glared at the yellow-haired one. "He told us the plan couldn't fail."

"Nor could it," agreed Jim. "Why do you think the Terrans go unarmed? They don't fear death. They know that their revenge would be too terrible to contemplate and they assume that you know it also." He glared at the agitator. "Shall I tell you what would happen? You would massacre the Terrans. Yes, you would take over the settlement, and then what? You would have several warehouses filled with goods. You would have a few weapons and limited ammunition; did any of you wonder from where you would receive more?"

"We would get it from the same place we received the Wilson guns," snapped the yellow-haired agitator. "We have friends."

"You would then have a pile of Terrans' corpses and valueless property, unless you are able to trade with Earth," Jim continued calmly. "Do you think, then, that you would rule Venus? No. The Council is not made up of fools. They know that Earth would want to avenge the outrage. They know that other ships will come. How best to show that they are as shocked as the Terrans? How else than by displaying a long line of corpses? Your corpses, and the half-breed question is settled for good."

His cold eyes stared over the crowd. "What position were you offered in the new regime?" he asked the yellow-haired man.

The man swallowed, stared at his neighbours, suddenly swung up his weapon. The thin tongue of flame seared across the hall, blinding in its brilliance. Jim ducked, dodged a second shot and swung up his own weapon. The Wilson gun spat. A finger of searing heat darted across the hall, hit, blinked out. A charred, smoking mass dropped to the floor, the melted ruin of a Wilson gun falling with a clang beside him.

Jim looked at the seared body. "He couldn't even shoot straight," he said. "What chance would you have against trained soldiers?"

The burly young man swallowed. He looked rather sick.

"What shall we do?" he asked humbly.

"Nothing," Jim snapped curtly. "Hide these weapons. They may be of use, but not until I order you. I have hopes that the question can be settled as it should be—by law and mutual agreement. One other thing. Who got you these guns I do not know, but I will venture a guess that he is of the pure strain. Ask yourselves, what do we stand to gain? Would he be after the highest position possible to a Venusian? Chief intermediary between Earth and Venus?"

He dropped the weapon, wiped the sweat from his face and neck. "Get me out of here," he gasped to Pheelan.

Gently the big half-breed led him into the open. The rain had stopped, the air smelling clean and sweet after the downpour which had washed it clear of the myriad floating spores from the giant fungi.

He stood, breathing deeply, his face haggard and strained. Beneath the long peak of his swept-back dark hair his face was pale. Automatically he fumbled for his pipe.

"I hated to do that, Pheelan," he muttered. "Killing that young fool. Who is at the bottom of it all?"

Pheelan shrugged.

"Still won't tell me?" Jim smiled, the pipe clenched between his teeth. "I leave tomorrow on the expedition. I'll probably be gone a week, maybe longer; it all depend on what we find. I rely on you to keep things under control until my return."

"I'll do that," Pheelan promised grimly. He caught Jim's arm. "Do you think that there is any hope?"

"I don't know. If only the Watchers would let me examine the records, enter the Anero Tanap..." he shrugged. "I'll do my best."

"How are you travelling?"

"Helicopter to the edge, then on foot. Fleetan's promised to fix a safe passage. We'll go via Elerdris, try to examine the archives there; but a lot depends on what we're allowed to do."

Pheelan grunted, dug one toe into the mud. "If you fail?" he asked.

"I fail," Jim laughed curtly. "I failed before, maybe I'll fail again. If I do, someone else will succeed, be sure of it."

"If you fail," Pheelan said slowly. "If you fail, then trouble will start."

"Not the garrison," snapped Jim sharply. "It would be suicide."

"Maybe not the garrison," said Pheelan suggestively. "There is something we can do nearer home. I've my daughter to think of; she's getting near marriageable age now. I want her to have free choice."

"Be careful," warned Jim seriously. "Be very careful. Remember the Watchers."

"I won't forget them," promised Pheelan, his great hands clenched. "I owe them something, when I think of my mother…" Anger swelled the thick veins of his neck.

"Take it easy," said Jim. He glanced at the now clear sky, the eternal layer of thick cloud, calm and fleecy after the recent storm. The sun, a great patch of golden light, had passed the zenith, was dropping towards the horizon. The thick drone of insects filled the suddenly quiet air.

"It's getting late," said Jim. Suddenly he snapped his fingers. "Daphne! I forgot her." He turned to Pheelan. "Take charge in there." He jerked his head towards the old warehouse. "Better get rid of the body. Bury it somewhere. I doubt if anyone will ask after him. If they do," he smiled grimly, "blame it on the Watchers."

Pheelan nodded, watched the Terran walk slowly down the narrow lane. He pulled at his lip, smiled a little, then suddenly squaring his shoulders, re-entered the warehouse.

Jim walked slowly, his feet dragging in the mud, his eyes vacant. He didn't notice the trimly clad members of the garrison until he had bumped into them, then it was too late.

He recognised the tall one, darted his eyes to each of the other two, felt quick relief.

"Excuse me," he muttered, trying to edge past.

"Not so fast," snapped the tall, dark-haired one. "Remember me?"

"Never seen you before," Jim said easily. "What do you want?"

"You're Warren, aren't you," said the tall man. "I remember you. You and that tavern-keeper beat me and my two friends up. Red's still in the sick bay. You smashed his face with that bottle, the other one has a broken jaw. I was lucky," he grinned savagely. "Now it's your turn."

"Are you sure this is the man, Tony?" One of the two men rubbed his jaw. "I thought that we were after that half-breed. I don't like beating up an Earthman."

"He's no Earthman," sneered Tony. "He's a renegade. Get him!"

He moved forward, his arms swinging at his side. Jim tensed. He dodged the first blow, weaving slightly and letting the fist pass over his shoulder. His own left sank into the tall man's stomach. His right hand, the edge stiffened, slashed across the exposed windpipe, the tall man retched and fell into the mud.

Then they were all over him. Desperately he struck, used his knees, feet, even butted with his head. He fell, struggled upright, slipped again, his arms pulling one of his foes down with him. He felt flesh near his mouth, bit savagely, someone yelled a vicious curse.

A fist crashed into his mouth and he tasted the warm salt of blood. Something ran down his forehead, blinding him. He drove his fist into a snarling mouth, felt teeth snap, felt a sharp pain in his knuckles. Desperately he floundered in the ankle-deep mud, trying to avoid the heavy boots. Tony swung at him.

He grabbed a foot, twisted, kept twisting. A man screamed with sudden agony, something snapped dully and the foot went limp. A boot thudded against his head. Something smacked against his nose, his mouth, his eyes. Dimly he realised that he was being beaten to a pulp.

He heaved, twisted, then suddenly the sun dimmed, stars flashed before him. He felt mud choking him, filling mouth and nose. Frantically he slewed in the mud, gagging. The shadow of a boot swung at him; he tried to dodge, couldn't, stared at it helplessly.

He never felt it land.

It was dark when he recovered consciousness. For a while he lay in the warm mud, trying to orient himself. Then, memory returning, he struggled to his feet. He ached all over, the knuckles of both hands were split, his nose broken.

Gingerly he touched his forehead, wincing as he felt various bumps and a jagged cut. He leaned for a while against a wall, then painfully staggered his way towards the lights of the House of Welcome.

His vision blurred as he walked, each step sending jolting throbs of agony stabbing through his broken head. Grimly he thought that he was lucky that he hadn't met the original three; he doubted if he would ever have walked again if he had. The thought of Red still in hospital gave him a savage satisfaction. Mentally he marked the tall Tony down for special attention.

He staggered as he reached the steps leading into the hotel. Darkness flooded over him.

CHAPTER SIX

SERPENT IN PARADISE

The vanes of the helicopter spun, the air blast flattening delicate fronds of lace-like vegetation. The sound of turbine rose to a shrill scream, the machine jerked, lifted, climbed into the air.

From the plastic cabin the young Terran pilot waved a gloved hand, circled once and vanished into the distance. Jim sighed and bent to examine the pile of baggage. He was still sore from the previous night's beating. His muscles ached, his eyes burned and every sharp sound made his head throb with more violent pain. Despite his injuries, he was smiling.

The smile died as he examined the pile of luggage.

"Who's bright idea was this?" he asked, jerking hand towards the heaped bundles.

"Mine, why?" Jack Conroy, elegant in his impeccable drill shirt and trousers, his high boots glistening, his jacket of fine leather fitting snugly around his slender waist, stared haughtily at the shabby figure of Warren.

"What did you hope to do with it?" Jim asked sarcastically. "Open a trading post?"

"No need to be clever about it," snapped Conroy. "If you'd been at the hotel last night instead of getting into a drunken brawl you could have advised us. As it was, we had to use our own discretion. What's the matter with it?

"As goods, nothing; but have you any idea how you going to carry it?"

"Fleetan said he would arrange for guides to meet us; I assumed the bearers would also be sent. After all, they can hardly expect us to carry our own things."

Jim breathed deeply, trying not to feel anger. "Tell me, Conroy," he said quietly, "have you the idea that Venus is something like old Africa? If you have, forget the notion. Venus isn't like that at all. The natives do not regard themselves as anyone's servants. They might agree to carry your stuff, but only because they wanted to, not for payment."

He bent over the pile, rapidly sorting the goods. "We don't need canned food," he snapped, tossing the packets to one side. "We don't need glasses, tableware, spare clothes, insect repellent, water purifier, stoves, shovels or tents." He opened a fresh bundle, turned scarlet at the sight of dainty feminine underwear.

"Perhaps you'd better sort your own things," he said to Daphne. "Keep the load to a minimum; we may have a long way to go."

"How about the weapons?" asked Professor Masters.

"Where are they?" Jim passed a hand across throbbing brows. "I must ask you to forgive me for last night. I intended to help you, but I met with an accident."

"Some accident!" Conroy sneered. Daphne darted him an exasperated look.

"For goodness sake keep quiet, Jack. Can't you see that Jim was seriously hurt?"

"Here are the weapons," interrupted the bearded professor. "I had a hard time persuading the port commander to let me have them."

Jim nodded. "I can imagine it." He ran an experienced eye over the guns. A long barrelled Wilson gun for each of the men. A stubby flame pistol for each of them, together with a broad bladed hunting knife in a sheath. Jim strapped the gun belt around his waist, adjusting knife and gun to comfortable, easy-to-reach positions.

"Just because we are armed, don't think that we intend shooting our way through," he warned. "Wait for my signal before you attempt to shoot. Under no circumstances make a threatening gesture with the guns towards any of the natives."

"Why not?" Conroy asked. He stared down the squat barrel of his pistol, aiming at imaginary targets.

"Because you'll be dead before you could ever pull the trigger," snapped Jim. "Take my word for it."

He swung a small pack to his shoulders, wriggling until the straps were comfortable. "Ready?"

"Aren't we going to wait here for our guides?" Daphne asked. She looked nervously at the mass of tangled vegetation stretching before them.

"No. They will find us when they want to. Anyway, we're in a hurry. I want to get to Elerdris as soon as possible."

"Why couldn't we fly all the way?" grumbled Conroy sweating beneath the weight of a bulging pack.

"Mutual agreement," explained Jim absently. "We have agreed not to encroach on the culture of the Venusians more than is necessary. There is an arbitrary line drawn around the area of the settlement, we call it the Edge, beyond which no aircraft or ground cars can go."

"Nonsense," snapped Conroy. "Do these people think that they can halt the march of progress?"

"I don't care what they think," Jim snapped. "All I know is that I want to be welcome at Elerdris. If we arrived by air we wouldn't be. Now shut up and keep moving!"

Steadily he plunged through the undergrowth, avoiding the boles of giant trees, warily stepping past swollen fungi, brushing aside tangled vines. Once he paused, listening, head cocked, one hand lifted for silence; then satisfied, he waved them on.

From time to time he squinted at an instrument strapped to his wrist, peered at the golden patch of the sun when it was visible between the tops of towering trees; around them insects droned in a buzzing swarm.

Conroy slapped at his neck, cursed, snapped irritably at Jim. "I thought that you said we didn't need repellent? I'm being eaten alive."

"Are you?" Jim asked seriously. "The insects rarely bite Terrans; something about our body-odour. Here!" he stepped to where a thick vine wreathed itself about the massive bole of a tree. With a slash of the keen knife he severed it, a thick yellow sap oozed from the cut.

"Rub yourself with this. The smell isn't very nice, but the insects won't bother you."

He waited while Conroy rubbed the thick mess over face, neck and hands. "How are you feeling?"

"Hot," admitted Daphne. "How far have we to go?"

"Several miles yet, I'm afraid. How about you, Professor? Feel like a rest?"

"Have we the time?" Masters rubbed at his beard. "I'd hate to spend the night in this environment."

"I think we can make time." Jim glanced at his wrist.

"I'll find a clearing. We can rest for a few minutes; have something to eat. We should take some salt pills, anyway." They walked steadily for another hour, then the jungle thinned before them. Thankfully, Daphne sat on a hillock of bare soil. "This is nice," she said gratefully. "Just like a little bit of paradise."

"You think so?" Jim smiled. "Like all paradises this has its serpent, also." He pointed to where a line of depressions led across the clearing. "The beast that made that belongs to no paradise. A relic of the Mesozoic period. A herbivore, of course, but an ill-tempered thing. It will attack anything moving within the range of its vision. Look at the trees; see how the vegetation has been stripped from them. There isn't a thing left for a height of over thirty feet. That will give you an idea how large it is."

"Are we in any danger?" Conroy asked, nervously fingering his Wilson gun.

"Not much. Luckily they are rare. The Venusians hate them. They ruin the plantations, smash the villages; make journeying hazardous. During the breeding season most of the natives stay out of the jungle. Even the Watchers are wary of them."

"What are these Watchers you keep mentioning?" Daphne asked. She bit into a succulent fruit Jim had found for her. He finished his own before answering.

"The Watchers? They watch, as you might have guessed from their name."

"That's all I'm going to tell you," said Jim calmly. He rose to his feet. "Time to be moving. Have you taken your salt pills?"

"Not yet," confessed Daphne. She swallowed several of the little white capsules, made a face, struggled into the straps of her pack. "Ready."

"Good," Jim glanced at the odd looking compass strapped to his wrist. "Let's step out now. We are behind time as it is."

They plunged into the jungle, moving in single file, Warren leading, setting a killing pace. He seemed worried, his eyes flickering over the tangled fronds ahead, jerking from side to side of the winding path he led. Daphne, following just behind, noticed the way he held the Wilson gun, finger on trigger, the long slender barrel menacing all before him. Wisely she bit back the questions she longed to ask, instead, she also walked with her hand resting near the butt of her pistol.

The stocky figure of the old professor moved next in line. He stared about him with rapt attention, pulling at his short beard, eyes gleaming with scientific interest from beneath bushy brows. He was careless of danger, the true scientist, interested to the exclusion of all else in his study of the variated botanical specimens through which they passed.

Conroy brought up the rear. He was nervous, twisting his head over his shoulder, irritably wiping sweat from face and neck. The trim shirt and trousers were dark and soggy with perspiration, his leather jacket swung unfastened, the straps of his bulging pack cut cruelly into the tender flesh. Suddenly he stopped.

"How about a rest?" he called.

"Not time," Jim yelled back. "Keep moving."

"I can't. I'm all in, this pack is cutting my arms off. I tell you I must rest."

Jim snarled impatiently, stopped, let the others catch up with him. "What's the matter this time?"

"I'm tired, that's what's the matter," snapped Conroy peevishly. "I say that we should have a rest, after all, Warren, we're not all used to marching through this heat."

"I suppose you're right," conceded Jim. "But we must make it a short one. It will be getting dark soon, and we have still some way to go." He glared at Conroy's bulging pack. "What on earth have you got in there, man?"

"Nothing I shan't need," defended the slim, effete Terran. "Some spare clothes, my toilet articles, a few books, a little medicine. Will you carry some of it?"

Jim held out his hand. "Give me the pack."

Surprised, Conroy handed it over. "Thank you."

"Don't thank me," snapped Jim. "I don't intend being your servant. Let me get rid of this junk." He opened the pack, shook the contents out onto the wet soil.

"What are you doing?" yelled Conroy, his pale face reddening with anger. "Leave those things alone."

Jim paid no attention. "As I thought," he muttered. "Two pairs of trousers, three shirts, spare jacket, spare pair of boots." Disgustedly he tossed them aside. "What's this?"

"Leave that alone," snapped Conroy. He stood, wide legged, the squat barrel of the flame pistol steady in his hand. "Touch that bundle, and I'll burn you down."

Jim rose slowly to his full height, his dark eyes blazed beneath his narrowed brows. "Put away that gun," he said quietly.

"Not until you move away from that bundle," Conroy repeated grimly.

Jim laughed silently. "You're out of character, Conroy," he said. "A man who loads himself with inessentials on a trip like this, to threaten his guide with a gun." He took a cautious step forward. "Put down that gun!"

"Not so fast," snapped Conroy. "Daphne, Masters, let us get one thing straight. Remember that it was my money that enabled you to come on this expedition. I did it for reasons you well know." His eyes rested on Daphne for a moment. "I don't intend some dirty renegade to boss me around, neither do I intend him to take the girl I love."

Jim let his eyes flicker to Daphne. "Is that true?"

"Never mind whether it's true or not," Conroy grated. "I've seen the way you look at each other, I won't stand for it. Now get away from that bundle."

"I see," Jim breathed. He smiled, let his hand gently move towards his holstered weapon. "Your love life doesn't interest me, but your insults do. You have a gun, Conroy, use it!" His hand darted towards the butt of the flame pistol.

Daphne screamed.

Something threshed in the near distance. Something huge, hissing snake-like as it sent small trees crashing to the soft loam. A nauseous odour wafted before it. The slither of scaly armour accompanied it, its very presence cast an aura of dread.

Something from the very depths of a tormented nightmare, thrust itself through the foliage above them.

Conroy screamed, swung the flame pistol, sent a livid shaft of burning chemical heat splashing against the slavering head of the giant reptile. Jim cursed, sprang for his Wilson gun, yelled at the stricken figure of the old professor.

"Get your Wilson. Get your gun, man. Quick!"

Desperately he snatched at his own weapon, swung the stock to his shoulder, squeezed the trigger. The thin line of brilliance cut a vivid path through the gloom of the jungle. It traced a delicate line from the flaring tip of the long barrel to one of the glittering jewel-like eyes. It struck, tore at the soft unprotected flesh, the smell of roasting meat caught at their nostrils.

The reptile screamed!

From the huge drooling mouth, red and lined with the flat teeth of a herbivore, from the depths of the long sinuous throat, the ghastly sound rang through the suddenly silent jungle. A sudden wave of noxious breath sent Jim staggering back, trying to control the violent retching of his stomach. From beside him a second Wilson gun spat scaring destruction. Jim wiped streaming eyes, grinned at Daphne.

"Aim at the eyes, then at just below the neck, in the hollow of the throat, but for God's sake mind his tail!"

Masters had reached his weapon and together the three of them sent tongue after tongue of searing heat at the giant monster. Even the incredible power of the Wilson gun hardly penetrated the thick armour of the nightmarish beast. Conroy, half insane with panic, was still blasting with his useless flame pistol.

"Conroy!" Jim called, straining his voice above the sounds of the guns and the savage thrashing of the beast. "Get out of the way! Stop shooting, and get out of way!"

Without waiting to see whether the man had obeyed his orders, Jim returned his attention to the great reptile. Despite all its terrible injuries, it still lived. The head was a charred mess, both eyes, and half the skull seared away by repeated blasts from the Wilson guns. Still the incredible vitality of the monster, its diverse nervous system, made it still dangerous.

Trees crashed as the thick tail swept viciously towards its tormentors. Lashing like the thong of a giant whip, the mass of flesh and bone swept all clear before it. Jim yelled a warning, flung himself to the soft ground, pulling Daphne beside him.

"Down Masters," he yelled. "For your life man, down!"

He stared in horror as the old professor made no move to safety. "Masters!" he screamed. "Masters, the tail! Watch the tail!"

With a whip-like motion the long armoured tail swept towards them. Desperately Masters, seeing his danger too late, tried to run. He was knocked from his feet, sent hurling against the bole of a giant tree, the Wilson spinning through the air after him.

Jim leapt to his feet, ran along close beside the terrible engine of destruction, and with the trigger of his weapon locked back, sent a continuous stream of searing death into the hollow of the great throat. Through armoured plates of bone, through flesh, through the very vitals and organs, the stabbing flame spat.

The beast was dead, had been for minutes now, but the reflex action of the great limbs sent the thick tail sweeping a path of danger. It slowed, jerked, rested quietly. Still Jim kept his finger locked on the trigger of the over-heated gun, not until the charges were exhausted did release the pressure, stagger weakly away from the huge mound of dead flesh.

Daphne turned a tear-stained face towards him.

"Jim," she pleaded. "My father. I think he's dead She broke into a fresh storm of weeping.

CHAPTER SEVEN

THE WATCHERS

Masters wasn't dead. As Jim gently lifted Daphne to one side he noticed with a quick flood of relief that the old professor still breathed. The blow from the great tail of the reptile had injured him, as had the impact with the bole of the tree, but he still lived.

"Is he dead, Jim?" Daphne asked dully.

"No," said Jim. "Knocked about a bit, but not too seriously."

"Are you sure?" she looked at him anxiously.

"Certain." He forced a confidence he did not feel into his voice. "Injured a little, that was to be expected, but he was lucky." He looked about him. "Where's Conroy?"

"Somewhere around," she answered listlessly, staring at the limp body of her father. "Why?"

"Find him, will you?"

"Do we need him?"

"Yes. Find him and bring him here. We shall have to carry your father, I can't do it alone."

He watched as she moved reluctantly away, then he bent over the prostrate figure of the old man. Gently he probed the shattered skull, noticed the flecks of blood at the corners of the mouth; tightened his lips in dismay. Obviously several ribs had been broken, one or more of them piercing the lungs. The injured skull told its own story of concussion and possible brain damage. Carefully moving the old professor, he noticed the left arm hanging limp, broken between elbow and shoulder. He straightened as he heard the approach of the other two.

"How is he?" Daphne asked.

"Not too good," Jim confessed. "Head injuries, a broken arm, and a good possibility of internal bleeding."

"Well," said Conroy. "This means the end of the expedition. We can't proceed with the professor in the state he is. We must return to the settlement."

"No!" protested Jim.

"No?" Conroy raised his eyebrows. "What else do you suggest?"

"We must carry him to Elerdris. It would be murder to take him back to the Edge. We'd have to wait days maybe for the helicopter. He would be dead before then."

"What else can we do?" Conroy insisted. "What good would it do him if we carry him to Elerdris? They have no hospital there. We would still have to get him to the settlement, and every minute we wait makes his chances of recovery less." He shook his head. "Sorry, Warren. I know how you feel, but I insist that we return to the settlement."

"We can't," Jim said flatly. He squinted at the dimming clouds, glanced at his wrist. "It will be dark soon. We could never get back through the jungle tonight. We'd have to camp in the open. What comfort can we give him? At Elerdris we can rest, I can head for the settlement tomorrow, or send a runner. I may be able to get permission for the helicopter to come for him. In any case we must get out of the jungle before dark."

"Why?"

"Several of the giant fungi spread their spores then. Most of them are quite harmless, but one or two are parasitic. If Masters should happen to breath one of those spores, let them settle on the internal wounds, then he will be dead before dawn." He shook his head. "We must get him to Elerdris."

Deliberately Jim drew his knife, cut down a couple of thin saplings, trimmed off the branching ferns. Lashing short pieces across head and foot, he quickly fashioned a rude stretcher.

Calmly he tied Conroy's spare clothing across the framework, making sure that all was firm. Sheathing the blade, he straightened.

"Help me get him on the stretcher." Conroy bit his lips, but made no effort to move. "Help me lift him man!" snapped Jim angrily. "Standing there won't solve anything!"

Slowly Conroy stepped forward.

"Now, gently, don't move him more than you have to. Daphne, you slip the stretcher beneath him as we lift. Ready?"

Daphne nodded, Conroy grunted.

"Right. Now!"

Gently they lifted the old man, Daphne slipping the rude stretcher beneath the limp figure. Jim adjusted Masters' head and limbs, lashing him firmly to the framework.

"Now," he grunted. "Move easily, and don't jolt him. I'll take the lead, Daphne can carry one of the guns and keep a look-out. I doubt if she will see anything, but we daren't take chances. Ready?"

With a smooth motion they lifted the stretcher, adjusted the weight, stepped carefully forward. Within ten steps they were sweating, within twenty Jim knew that they would never make it.

Grimly he plodded on through the darkening jungle. The stretcher dragged at his arms, his eyes burned with trying to watch every place where he might rest a foot. He knew how slender was the old man's hold on life. One slip, a fall, and the jagged edges of the broken ribs would slash the lungs to ribbons. He hoped that Daphne hadn't thought of that.

She strode beside the unconscious body of her father, the Wilson gun dragging from her hand, her eyes showing the strain under which she moved. From time to time she glanced at the sweat-gleaming face of Conroy, then at the sturdy shoulders of Warren, tensed and stubborn as he grimly set the pace. Once she made as if to speak, then bit her lips and kept silent.

Insects droned about them, from the far distance something screamed, nearer, a giant fungi exploded with a soft plop emitting a cloud of brown spores. She looked over her shoulder, and stepped closer to Warren.

"I think someone's watching us," she whispered. "I keep getting the feeling that someone is just beyond range of vision, or has just dodged behind a tree."

Jim grinned tightly. "It's probably the Watchers," he explained. "Don't worry about them."

"The Watchers?" Daphne frowned. "What is this mystery of the Watchers? Why won't you tell me?"

"Later," Jim said. "How is your father?"

"I don't like it," she said worriedly. "There's blood on his lips, that means torn lungs doesn't it? His colour isn't too good, and he's shivering. What can we do?"

"Cover him as best we can. Here." Carefully Jim slipped off his leather jacket, letting her hand hold one side of the stretcher as he removed his hand. "Put this over him, get Conroy's jacket, use your own too. We won't need them."

"How about a rest?" Conroy called softly. Like Daphne, he too had the feeling that someone was watching them. Instinctively he lowered his voice.

"Maybe we'd better," agreed Jim. "Set it down gently." Thankfully he straightened, easing cramped muscles. "I'll try to get some fruit. Keep a close watch Daphne, but remember, don't threaten anything with the Wilson gun. Don't lift or aim it unless you intend to fire, then shoot, and shoot straight." He vanished into the undergrowth.

Conroy cleared his throat nervously. "Do you think we can trust him?"

"Trust him?" Daphne looked her surprise. "Of course we can. Why do you ask?"

"Well, look at it this way. Warren is obviously determined to continue with the expedition. Even though he knows that your father is going to die, yet he won't return to the settlement. I'm suspicious. I'd like to know why."

"Who says that father is going to die?" Daphne demanded desperately.

Conroy smiled pityingly. "What do you think? He has internal injuries hasn't he? Look at the colour of his face. How can we get medical aid for him where we're going? If we had returned immediately to the settlement, he'd have stood a chance. As it is…" He shrugged.

"Jim said that he would return to the settlement, bring the helicopter to Elerdris to pick up father," Daphne protested. "You must agree that would be the most sensible thing to do."

"If he does it," admitted Conroy. "But what's to prevent him going off and leaving us at Elerdris? How would we ever know where he had got to? He could go where he intends going, then say he got lost, that he had an accident, even say nothing at all." He grimaced.

"Warren's almost a native. He could live in the jungle for years if he had to. I tell you, I don't trust him!"

"Well I do!" Daphne said hotly. "He has given us no reason for not trusting him, and he is the only one we can rely on now."

Conroy's face hardened. "So you trust him?" he sneered. "A man with his reputation, a drunkard, a renegade, a man despised by every Terran on Venus. Fleetan warned me about him. The Port Commander warned us both. I know why you trust him, you romantic little fool!"

"What do you mean?" Daphne asked quietly.

"You've let a cheap reputation make you lose your sense of judgment," Conroy spat. "Oh, I've been watching you. The way you look at him, the way you touch his hand at times. Do you think I'm blind?"

Daphne flushed. "What you are saying isn't true, and you know it. Jim doesn't think anything of me."

"But you do of him," Conroy lowered his voice. "Listen darling, you know how I feel about you, you've known for a long time now. We were to be married after this expedition, remember? I only agreed to finance it because it meant so much to you and to your father. Don't let me down for the sake of a momentary infatuation. How would you feel if you married Warren? What would people say?"

"I don't know," said Daphne. "I don't know—and I don't care."

Something rustled in the undergrowth. Startled, Daphne swung the long barrel of the Wilson gun, her finger tensing on the trigger.

"Don't shoot," called Jim. "It's me. Warren." He stepped from the undergrowth, holding a great pile of fruit in his arms. Dropping them in front of the others, selected a small, hard-rinded nut-like globe. Slashing the tough skin with his knife, he squeezed a thick golden sap from the cut, tasted it, nodded, and stepped to the side of the unconscious man.

"What are you doing?" called Daphne.

"It will help," Jim said quietly. He dripped the sap onto Masters' lips. "The juice has a soporific effect. It will serve in lieu of an anaesthetic, without any harmful effects." He stepped back. "Hurry and eat, we must on our way."

"What are you going to do when we reach Elerdris?" Daphne asked.

Jim looked at her oddly. "That rests with how we are received."

But...?" Daphne commenced, then lapsed into silence. She had just remembered that sounds carried far in the jungle. She wondered if Jim had heard her and Conroy talking. Savagely she bit into one of the fruits.

Conroy wiped his lips, leaned back against the bole of a tree. "How much farther have we to go, Warren?"

"Not too far. Why?"

"I was wondering if it would be possible to send off a runner tonight. If we could, we might be able to have the helicopter pick up Masters tomorrow."

Jim shook his head.

"Why not?" demanded Conroy. "The old man's in a bad way. I think he's dying. If we can get him to hospital he may have a chance. As it is he has none. For Daphne's sake we must do what we can."

"Then why don't you use your radio?" Jim asked quietly.

Conroy blushed, then to cover his confusion, blustered. "Radio? What do you mean?"

"I mean the portable radio you have in your pack," Jim explained quietly.

"I haven't got a radio."

"No?" Jim grinned savagely. Stepping to where the bundles had been tossed he lifted his foot. "Then you have no objection to my stamping on your bundle?"

"Certainly I have. Who do you think you are? I warned you once, Warren, I'll not do it again. Touch that bundle and I'll burn you down."

"What with?" Jim said coldly. "You were so panic-stricken a short while ago, that you didn't realise that you had lost your pistol. Now. Do you object?"

Conroy whitened with rage. "Keep your dirty feet off my property," he snarled.

"Do you have a radio, Conroy?" Daphne asked hopefully.

"He has," Jim said quietly. "I noticed it when I threw out his things. A limited range, single wavelength job." He smiled without humour. "How much did Fleetan promise you to report our every move, Conroy?"

"What are you talking about?"

"You know what I mean," snapped Jim. His hand flickered to his belt, returned weighted with a flame pistol. "Now, Conroy, talk. What did Fleetan want you to do?"

"Nothing."

The squat barrel made an arc through the humid air. Conroy cried out, cowered, put his hands protectively to his cheek. The scarlet welt of the blow stood startling clear against the pallid skin.

"Talk!" snarled Jim. "Talk or I'll beat your face to pulp. How much?"

"Twenty thousand," muttered Conroy.

"For what?"

"To tell him where we were, and what you had discovered."

"When were you to use the radio?"

"On our return," Conroy quivered. "Don't hit me, Warren. I didn't see any harm in letting him know."

"You wouldn't," Jim snapped contemptuously. Deliberately he swung the flame pistol, sent a searing blast of fire stabbing from the squat muzzle. The pack flared for a moment, something compact and metallic spluttered then ran in molten ruin. Daphne screamed, then cried in protest.

"Jim! The radio, we could have used it, saved father!"

"We could have used it," admitted Jim. "Yes. We wouldn't have saved anyone."

He holstered the flame pistol. "Listen, Conroy," he said quietly. "You should have told me that you had a radio. Fleetan ordered you not to, was that it?"

Conroy nodded.

"I thought so. Do you know what would have happened had you tried to use it? I thought not. You would have died, Conroy. We all would have died. Fleetan knew that."

"But why, Jim?" Daphne said angrily. "Why would we have died?"

"The Watchers would have killed us," explained Jim simply. "We entered the jungle, left the settlement, by special arrangement. That is why we didn't come all the way by helicopter. We must keep to that arrangement, or pay the penalties for breaking it. We are allowed no recording equipment. I would have taken a chance on that. We are not allowed radio. I refuse to risk certain discovery of its use."

He laughed at Conroy. "Twenty thousand credits! He could have offered a million, you would never have lived to collect them."

A moan from the injured man jerked them around. Jim strode across to the stretcher, bent over it, another of the nut-like fruits in his hand. The moaning died.

"Come on, Conroy," Jim ordered. "Our differences can wait. We must get him to Elerdris. Ready?"

Together they lifted the stretcher, commenced the gruelling march, necks and arms aching in anticipation. It had grown darker, great patches of shadow clustering about the boles of the giant trees, hiding the pitfalls in the soft loam of the jungle floor. Jim began to sweat, thinking of the possibility of a fall. If he should slip, break an ankle… He gritted his teeth, forced himself not to think of it. It was best not to anticipate.

Daphne led the way, striding carelessly over the tangle of vines and fronds covering the soft dirt. She set a hard pace, fear of the dark, of the silent watching jungle lengthening her stride. She held the Wilson gun at her hip, her slender fingers tight around the stock, the knuckles white beneath the strain.

A fungus popped, another, then a third. A sickly odour hovered in the air, then was gone as they passed the cloud of floating spores. Jim bit his lips worriedly, glanced over his shoulder at the unconscious man, then jerked his gaze ahead as he felt his foot slipping on a rotted vine.

Daphne was now several paces ahead, she slipped between two trees, disappeared from immediate view. A scream lanced through the thick air. Another! Another!

The Wilson gun thundered a savage blast.

CHAPTER EIGHT

ELERDRIS

Jim swore, automatically lunged forward, the weight of the stretcher jerking him back. Swiftly he set his end down on the loam, and snapped orders to the trembling figure of Conroy.

"Stay by him. Don't leave this spot." He raced between the two trees, tugging at the flame pistol.

Barely had he cleared them, than he bumped heavily into Daphne. For an instant she struggled, then collapsed sobbing into his arms.

"What is it?" he snapped, eyes probing the jungle, flame pistol steady in his hand.

"There, Jim," she explained shakily. "I saw it as I left the trees, I screamed, fired, and then you came."

Jim followed her pointing finger, despite himself shudders ran up his spine.

A man hung from a low branch. He spun gently, the rope around his neck twisting his head, giving him a queer lopsided look. He hadn't died easily. The rotting spots on his body, the grimace of intense agony, the starting eyes, all told their mute story. Jim cautiously approached the swinging figure, Daphne treading on his heels.

"Why," she said in amazement. "I've seen him before. He was the merchant we bought those things from in the market."

Jim nodded, gazing at the strangely scarred forehead. The man hadn't died from the rope. He had met death some other way. Jim studied the naked body, noticed the tiny pinpricks, the faint fuzz of golden fungus already growing on the dead flesh.

He stepped back, holstering the flame pistol. "Come on. Daphne," he said quietly. "We can't do anything for him, and he can't hurt us."

Conroy still stood by the stretcher. His eyes looked wild in the deepening gloom of the jungle, his hand groped at his empty holster. "What was it?"

"A dead man," Jim explained laconically. "Ready?"

"Wait a minute," snapped Conroy. "What do you mean, a dead man? Are we safe here? The killer could get us just as easily, more so laden as we are with the stretcher."

"They won't hurt us," Jim said quietly. "It was something quite personal, you have no need to fear. Just pick up your end, and follow me. Ready, Daphne?"

"If you say so, Jim," she said nervously. "But I don't like it."

"And neither do I," snapped Conroy. "There's too much mystery about the whole thing. Who killed that man? Why? I want to know."

"So do I," Daphne supported. "Why don't you tell us, Jim? We are as much concerned as you are."

He looked at them, hesitated, then shrugged. "If you insist," he said quietly. "I'll tell you. That man was killed by the Watchers."

"The Watchers!" snorted Conroy. "Always the Watchers. Who are these mysterious Watchers?"

Jim sighed, "They are watching us now, they have been from the very moment we left the settlement. They will until we return there. They are everywhere."

He gestured towards the dark jungle. "Somewhere in that mass of undergrowth, a man is watching. He is white. White-haired, white-skinned, red-eyed. A Venusian. His body is daubed with green and yellow, his hair bound. He is a master of camouflage. He is armed. Not with a Wilson gun or a flame pistol, but with a short blow-pipe and a handful of poisoned darts. He is an expert shot. He is a Watcher."

"A murderer!" snapped Conroy.

"No. A Watcher," corrected Jim. "They are not murderers. The man swinging dead from that tree, was not murdered. He had been warned, the scar on his fore head served as a constant reminder to him to stay out of the jungle, to stay in the settlement. The half-breeds don't need a scar, they know the penalty too well."

"I begin to understand," murmured Daphne. "A kind of police force."

"More than that," agreed Jim. "They are picked from the cream of Venus. They serve as their own judge, jury, and executioner. They know everything, their means of communication is something that has never been explained. They punish all crime, they safeguard the individual, they are never seen, but they see everything."

"I see," said Conroy. He picked up his end of the stretcher. "Let's get out of this damn jungle!"

They passed the swinging corpse, Daphne averting her eyes. They winded their tortuous way between the boles of the night shrouded trees, past unhealthy looking fungi, picking a careful passage among the twisted vines. Once Jim paused, head cocked, frowning. He shrugged, commenced the march again. The unconscious man began to moan in his agony.

Again Jim paused, set down the end of the stretcher, lifted a hand for silence. Something moved in the jungle ahead of them. Something treading a soft passage through the tangled undergrowth, silently Jim drew his flame pistol.

A man appeared before them. A tall native, his long fine hair rippling down his shoulders. Another followed him, then several more. Jim holstered the pistol, took the Wilson gun from Daphne's quivering fingers; raised his empty hand in the sign of peace.

"The night is near," said the leader in perfect Terran. He was an old man, with a calm unruffled expression. He didn't appear to notice Conroy's hand stealing towards his knife.

"The dark time is upon us," replied Jim in the same sonorous mode of speech. "We are travellers, travelling in peace, bound for the village of Elerdris. One of our number received injuries," he flickered his eyes warningly towards Conroy.

"I heard of your combat with the great reptile," said the old man. "For that we are indebted. I have with me young men, men who are not fatigued with journeying. May they relieve you of your burden?"

"It would be a gracious gesture," said Jim calmly. He watched as two sturdy young men swung the stretcher to their shoulders. Conroy plucked at his sleeve.

"Give me a weapon," he hissed. "I don't like this. How did the old man know we had killed that beast?"

"They know," answered Jim curtly. "Keep your hand from that knife, remember the Watchers. If you tried to draw a threatening weapon, you would be dead before it had levelled in your hand. These people have their own escort."

He fell into step beside the old man. "We had hoped for your company on our journey from the Edge," he said casually. "One high on the Council had agreed to arrange it.

"Fleetan," the old man smiled. "Some such had been requested, but the great beast in the jungle made travel difficult." He did not apologise for failing to carry out Fleetan's orders.

Jim nodded. "How far is it to Elerdris?"

"Not far, you would call it an hour. What is wrong with the one who is carried?"

"Grave injuries," Jim explained seriously. "His head is broken. His arm, and I fear that many internal organs are damaged. I doubt if he will live."

"He did well in the combat," mused the old man. "It may be that we could assist him. Have I your permission to treat the injuries?"

"Mine, yes," said Jim. "But there are others, his friend, his daughter. I must ask them."

Conroy was openly sceptical. Daphne worried.

"How can they treat father, Jim?" she asked. "A primitive people like these can't know anything of surgery. What would they use for anaesthetics, sutures, transfusions?" she shook her head. "No, Jim. I can't allow it. We must get father back to the settlement hospital."

"We can't," Jim was brutally frank. "Listen to me, Daphne. I know how seriously your father is hurt. He will die before he can ever reach the hospital. The journey alone would kill him. If you refuse, then you are killing him. At least why not give them a chance?"

"Those natives?" Conroy sneered. "Witch doctors to cure broken ribs. Why don't you grow up, Warren? Who are you trying to fool?"

"Have we any choice?" Jim asked coldly.

"What do you think is best, Jim?" Daphne pleaded. "I can't hope that these people can help father, but what else can I do?"

"Nothing," Jim was deliberately curt. "Either these people help him, or we watch him die. Which would you prefer, Daphne?"

"You know what I must say," she said blinking back her tears. "But, Jim. Remember he's my father, I want to trust you, but he must come first."

"I understand," Jim said bitterly. "If he dies, then I get the blame. Is that it?"

"Yes," snapped Conroy. "If you hadn't smashed the radio, we could have called for help. You did that and you must pay for it if anything goes wrong."

"You've a short memory," reminded Jim savagely. "Have you forgotten that man swinging from a tree?"

"We have only your word for the existence of these mysterious Watchers," Conroy snapped. "I doubt if your tale would sound reasonable at an investigation."

Jim shrugged, left them, moved to the head of the little column next to the old man.

"Have your friends decided?"

"We beg that you, as our host, will extend to our sick the comfort of your treatments," Jim said dully.

"It shall be done," answered the old man. He seemed to be secretly amused.

They left the jungle as the last rays of the sinking sun threw a pale golden light on the tops of the towering trees. Behind them, the rank growth of the matted vegetation hummed with the drone of night insects, and the frequent popping of the bloated fungi. Before them, a cleared stretch of grassland sloped to the village. Jim breathed a deep sigh of relief.

"Elerdris," said Jim, dropping back to walk beside Daphne. "The nearest village to the settlement, but they are all much alike."

"What do they live on?" Daphne asked interestedly.

"Tree fruits mostly. Some edible fungi, and certain saps, fermented and otherwise. The natives are vegetarians."

"How about the industries?"

"None. The climate makes fires unnecessary, also the manufacture of clothing. They wear a single robe, a breech cloth, or something similar. There is no mining, aside from a few metals easily obtained from outcroppings, they use none. Most things are made from hard woods, ceramics, and a kind of plastic. The life is what you would primitive, but not when you look a little more closely it."

"How do you mean?"

"Primitives usually live in dirt. Not so the Venusians. They know the value of hygiene, of a proper well-balanced diet, and they aren't saddled with ridiculous taboos."

"No?" Daphne smiled a little. "What of the Watchers?"

"They aren't superstitious nonsense. They are grim reality." His hands tightened. "The Watchers have a lot to answer for, not all of it good."

Daphne looked at him, surprised at the sudden tightness of his voice. She said nothing, but her eyes were gentle.

They had reached the outskirts of the village. Low houses of wood and stone each set in its own ground of well-tended garden. Larger huts towards the centre of the village, and one towering building fashioned of stone soared upwards from the exact centre.

Daphne looked about her, frowning. "Something is missing," she said wonderingly. "Something doesn't seem normal."

"No dogs," snapped Conroy. "Ever seen a native village before without dogs?"

"It isn't only that," insisted Daphne. "Something doesn't seem right."

Jim smiled. "You miss the children," he explained. "And you miss the gaping crowds. Venusians aren't like the primitives of Earth."

"You mean that they aren't curious?" Daphne asked incredulously.

"They're curious enough," said Jim. "But they're good-mannered too. They don't have to gape at us, touch our things, make an exhibition of their visitors. The rules of good behaviour are very strong, every native knows them, and so should every Terran."

As their guide halted before a low hut, he gestured apologetically. "My home. I bid you welcome. Refreshments will be offered in due course, now I must see that your injured companion receives such comfort as can be given."

"I must go with him," Daphne insisted.

"That is not possible," the old man said firmly.

"I must go with him. He will need me," Daphne sounded desperate. Jim took her arm.

"He knows what he is doing," he reassured her. "Trust him. You are tired and hungry, your father is in good hands. There is nothing more we can do for him." He smiled at the old man as he led Daphne within the hut. "You will return soon?"

"Soon," promised the Venusian. He gestured, turned, and followed the stretcher-bearers down the street towards the towering building.

The hut was clean with a minimum of furnishings. The main outer room held a table, several chairs, and a great bowl of fragrant flowers. Several woven mats hung against the walls, the windows were glazed with a transparent plastic. They did not examine the inner rooms.

Jim slumped into one of the soft chairs, realising for the first time just how tired he was. His muscles ached from carrying the stretcher, and from his beating. His nose hurt, and his head throbbed. Reaction from the strain of guiding them to the village sent tremors through the long muscles of legs and arms.

Conroy too showed signs of strain. He kept twitching, shifting restlessly in his seat, striding up and down the tamped earth floor. Daphne sat silent, only the nervous twining of her fingers betraying the strain she was under.

A man came from one of the inner rooms, he bore a bowl of fruits, a flat cake of some dry powdery substance, and a container filled with green wine. He set the food and drink on the table, gestured invitation, and as silently withdrew.

"Time to eat," announced Jim. He poured a goblet of wine, gulped it down, refilled it. He grinned at looks the others gave him.

"Don't get prudish," he warned. "The wine constitutes a part of the balanced diet—in moderation of course."

Daphne tasted a little of the crumbling cake-like substance. "What is it?"

"A paste made from various crushed nuts," explained Jim. "High protein value, eat some." He broke off a piece, selected one of the fruits, began eating hungrily. After a moment's hesitation the others followed his example.

The meal finished, Jim groped for his pipe, lit it, sent fragrant clouds coiling towards the ceiling. He pulled container of wine closer to his elbow, propped up his feet, and sighed luxuriously.

Conroy sneered. "Instead of swilling that wine, how about finding out how the professor is? Or don't you care?"

Daphne cried out in protest. Jim's face darkened.

"You have to be clever don't you, Conroy? You have to cause trouble. What's the matter? Aren't you important enough on Venus?"

Conroy surged forward, lips drawn back from teeth in an animal-like snarl, hands clenched into fists. "Damn you, Warren," he snarled. "I've stood all I intend to from you. You dirty renegade!" he swept up the heavy container of wine, threw it with all the strength of his arm.

Jim tried to duck, the soft chair hampered him, prevented quick movement. He flung up an arm, the heavy container numbed his elbow, cracked against his temple. Wine and blood ran down the side of his face. He threw himself sideways, rolling out of the chair as he hit the floor. Conroy rushed at him, swinging his heavy boot.

Daphne screamed. Jim rolled desperately from the path of the vicious kick, grunted as the boot thudded against his sore ribs, tried to grab it, failed as his fingers slipped off the mud covered leather. Conroy grinned savagely drew back his foot for a second blow. Sick and numbed, Jim knew that he could never avoid it.

It never landed. Surprised, Jim lunged to his feet, drew back his fist, let his hand fall to his side.

The old Venusian had entered the room.

CHAPTER NINE

MELIK

He stood just within the door, an old man, yet he radiated a vitality seldom seen even in the very young. His eyes blazed in the alabaster whiteness of his face, the red-tinted orbs staring at the suddenly silent Conroy. To Jim, it almost seemed that the blazing eyes emitted visible force.

For a moment they stood there—Daphne, her hand half raised to her lips to stifle a scream; Conroy, his hands still clenched, his eyes glittering with hatred; Jim, fist tensed by his side, breathing deeply with the pain of his injuries. He was the first to move.

"How is the injured man?" he asked.

"Well," replied the Venusian. He closed his eyes, and when he opened them again, the feral blazing energy had gone. "He rests within the house of healing. Others are with him. Soon he will be well."

"Are you sure?" cried Daphne.

"He will be well," repeated the old man. He stared at Conroy. "Tonight you are a guest. Tomorrow you will return from whence you came. Enter the jungle again at your peril, the Watchers will be notified."

"Good," snapped Conroy. "You will come with me of course, Daphne. We will bring out the helicopter, take your father to the settlement hospital." He stared at Jim. "This means the end of the expedition of course. I never did think that your wild ideas had a basis of fact, now I'm sure of it."

"I'm not returning with you, Jack," Daphne said.

"You're not? But you must, Daphne. I want you to. We can be married at the settlement, live there until your father is fit to travel. What else can you do?"

"I'm staying here. Here with my father. I trust these people, Jack. I don't want you to take him back to the settlement."

Conroy's face hardened. "You return with me, Daphne, or our engagement is finished. I shall withdraw my financial support for this expedition, you know what that means."

"You think it means that we shall be stranded," said Daphne calmly. "Maybe we shall be, but return to Earth at your price just isn't worth it."

"But what about our engagement, Daphne?" Conroy asked wildly. "Have you lost all feeling for me? You loved me once. Has a new face, a cheap story-book adventurer, made you forget all we meant to each other? Come with me darling. When we return to Earth, you'll never regret it. I promise you."

"No, Jack," Daphne held out her hand, a thin gold band containing a single glittering stone resting on the palm. "I'm sorry, but this is the end between us. Here." She tossed the ring onto the table. It glittered in the fitful light of the primitive lamp.

Conroy stared at it, stared at her, then with a snarl swept the ring into his pocket. The door to one of the inner rooms banged behind him. Jim sighed.

He searched for his pipe, looked ruefully at the shattered stem, replaced it with one he carried in a shirt pocket. He poured water from a jug into an unglazed bowl of earthenware, and he dipped his head, wincing as he washed the cut on his temple. When he had dried himself he noticed that a fresh container of wine stood on the table. He smiled his thanks at the old Venusian.

"The host is gracious to his guests," he spoke the stilted form of speech beloved by nearly all the unspoilt natives.

"The guest is tired. It is the pleasure of the host to provide for his guests." The old man gestured invitation. Jim poured a generous measure, drank the thick wine gratefully.

"Why have you come to Elerdris?"

"Why?" Jim smiled. "I had hoped to be allowed to examine your records. I am a seeker after truth. I know that your archives would assist me greatly."

"You know of the true tongue?"

"I am a Terran," explained Jim. "I have had no opportunity of learning the speech of your people."

"Then how will the records help you?"

"Mathematics are universal. I believe that the men of Venus and the men of Earth are related. I believe that, many thousands of years ago, men set forth from Earth in ships of space, even as we do now. That they landed on Venus, became your forebears. I would like to prove this theory."

"And you think that the records could help you?"

"Nothing else will." Jim sighed, drank at his wine. "I've tried everything I can think of to find the truth. Once I almost had it, then things went wrong." He grinned at his host. "You probably know all about it."

"Yes," the old man nodded gravely. "I am custodian of the archives here in Elerdris," he said calmly. "I am able to grant what you seek. When will be a convenient time for your examination?"

"Tomorrow," said Jim quickly. "At dawn."

"At dawn," agreed the old man. He rose, saluted them gravely, vanished into the insect-droning night. Jim released his breath in a deep sigh.

"What do you think of that?"

"Luck," Daphne sat close to him at the table. "Tell me, Jim. Has anything struck you as peculiar?"

"How do you mean?"

"Well, you tried to examine the records before didn't you?"

Jim nodded.

"You couldn't then. Now, for some reason, they are letting you. Why?"

"Maybe Fleetan had something to do with it."

"No. That old man wouldn't take orders from Fleetan," she frowned. "You didn't see what happened when he came in the but and found Conroy trying to kill you, I did. He just looked at him. Jack went all stiff. I tried to scream but I couldn't—it was as if something held me. And what about that man we saw on the trail, the dead man? He had something to do with us, I'm sure of it. Why was he killed?"

"I don't know," said Jim impatiently. "He could have been killed for any one of a dozen reasons. I'm not interested. All I want to do is to examine those records." He bit at his lower lip. "I wish we had a camera, could photograph them."

"Jim," said Daphne. "Tell me honestly. Can you speak Venusian?"

"No."

"Are you sure that you're telling the truth?"

"I should know," snapped Jim. "Why do you ask?"

"No reason," she rose. "Will I be allowed to examine the records with you?"

"I don't know. Do you want to?"

"Naturally," she smiled. "After all I am a member of this expedition, and I would like to see them. Will you arrange it, Jim?"

"If I can."

"It is very important that I see them, Jim," Daphne insisted. "Very important."

For a moment their eyes stared into each other's. Blue into brown, each trying to read the other's secrets. Daphne laughed, slipped from the table.

"Goodnight, Jim."

"Goodnight," he said absently. The door of the second inner room closed behind her. Jim rested his head on his arms, smoking quietly, busy with his thoughts. He sat for a long while before going to bed.

He awoke with a throbbing head, stiff and sore from his exertions and the beatings he had received. For a while he lay on the narrow pallet, staring at the low ceiling, trying to arrange his thoughts. A sound from Daphne's room jerked him to the business at hand. A jug of water stood by the earthenware bowl. He carefully washed his face and hands, then poured the remainder of the water over his naked torso. He was buttoning his shirt when Daphne entered the room.

"Dressed yet?"

"Just a second." He slipped on his jacket, adjusted the belt holding the holsters for the flame pistol and knife. Automatically he checked the loading of the pistol, grinned at Daphne.

"I feel a fool carrying this thing around, like an aborigine with a spear in Greater New York. Better take it I suppose. Where's Conroy?"

"Gone."

"Already?"

"They came for him just before you awoke. The old man, his name is Melik by the way, and two young ones. I didn't speak to him."

"How did you know the old man's name?"

"He told me, and Jim! He said that father was much better, and that I could examine the records with you." She flushed a little. "I hope that you didn't mind my asking him?"

"Of course not," Jim glanced at the table. "How about breakfast?"

"Fruit, nut paste and wine," Daphne looked at Jim as he poured from the beaker. "Must you, Jim?"

Deliberately he drank, refilled the goblet, drank again. Flushing, she sat down, began to gnaw at one of the fruits. "Aren't you eating?"

"No." He stood, pipe in mouth, wine goblet in hand staring out of one of the windows. The light of the new day shone on his hair, accentuating the whiteness of his skin, the startling contrast of his brown hair and eyes. The dark blotches of bruises and the ugly cut on his temple showed clearly. Daphne's eyes softened as she watched. "Sorry, Jim," she apologised.

"What for?"

"For criticising your drinking."

"Forget it. Here comes Melik."

The old man entered the hut. "Have you rested?"

"We have. Has the host?"

"The host has rested," replied the old man sonorously. "Shall we go?"

Together they left the hut. Daphne stared curiously at the villagers strolling quietly about their business. She frowned.

"Jim. Where are the children?"

"The children are in a place of their own," explained Jim. "They are in a sort of communal creche. Don't stare at the people, Daphne. It is considered bad manners to display curiosity."

"Sorry," she flushed, walked with her eyes firmly before her. Jim grinned, touched her hand.

"You look like a little girl who has just been scolded. Sorry to snap at you, but my nerves are on edge."

Automatically she squeezed his hand, a faint reddening of his pale cheeks betrayed his discomposure. Hastily she released the pressure of her fingers.

Melik halted before a fairly large building. Around it stretched a wide expanse of well-tended lawn. Flowers bloomed in profusion, sending their exotic perfume to hang on the humid air.

"Our house of healing," explained Melik. "Your father is within would you care to see him?"

"May we?" Daphne glanced at Jim.

"If Melik says we may, I can see no harm."

They followed the old man along a path of crushed stone to the single low doorway. Melik lifted a hand warningly.

"Make no sound, watch, but do not speak," he swung open the carved panel.

A large room stretched before them. Cots lined the walls, empty, but clean and obviously ready for immediate use. A group of Venusians sat around the farthest bed. They all faced towards the centre of a circle. All seemed wrapped in deepest concentration. All were men.

Masters lay on the cot in the centre of the circle. He seemed to be asleep, a healthy colour on his stubbled cheeks, the short beard he affected had been washed and combed. His arm had been splinted, bandages covered his forehead, a loose garment covered him from neck to feet. He had no other covering.

Jim touched Daphne's arm, gestured, smiled reassuringly. Mindful of Melik's warning, he did not ask any of the questions that came thronging to his lips. Silently they left the building.

"How did you set the ribs?" he asked the old man when they were outside. "As I remember it, his internal injuries were pretty bad."

"We have our methods," smiled the Venusian. "The group around him are in close rapport. To break their concentration would have serious results. They are lending him their strength." He walked on in silence. Jim knew better than to question his meaning.

Before them, the high towering building reared, the stonework of its structure making his eyes widen as he noticed the perfect precision of the joints. A high arched doorway, fitted with panels of deeply carved wood, opened as they approached. A young Venusian watched them with intent eyes, vanishing within the building at a gesture from Melik.

"The records are within," the old man said. He seemed to hesitate. "I have agreed for the young Terran lady to examine with you. I ask you if you have any device for recording what you have seen. I believe that such instruments are common on your world."

"They are," agreed Jim. "But we have no such instrument with us."

"It is well. Enter then, the youth will show you what you require. I will meet you when the sun is overhead." He lifted his arm in salute, turned, strode away. Jim looked at Daphne.

"This is it," he said drawing a deep breath. "I hope that you have a good memory, we're going to need it." Taking her arm, he led her within the wide-flung doors.

A stone floor stretched before them, almost the full width of the building, the young Venusian waited for them. He bore a great bundle of thin metal plates, setting them down on a low table, he gestured, retreated to the end of the hall. Reverently Jim picked up one of the plates. As he had suspected it was of metal. From its weight he guessed it to be of gold. It was covered with script, what appeared to be equations and close set rows of tables. The lines had been etched with some acid. He put it down.

"We must start from the beginning," he whispered to Daphne. "I assume that they are in chronological order. I'll scan them, then pass them to you. Try to remember any drawings, equations, mathematical formulae that you can." He sighed. "To examine these properly would take a lifetime, we have a few hours, let's not waste any of it."

They set to work.

Frantically Jim let his eyes race over the plates, trying to decipher the close set columns of script, the various equations. As he read them, a frown gathered on his forehead. Irritably he set the plate down, picked up another.

"What's wrong?" Daphne asked. She put down the plate she was holding, after giving it what appeared to be no more than a casual glance.

"I thought that I could read this stuff," whispered Jim. "I can't."

"Try looking, at the later ones, then work backwards," suggested Daphne. "The style of writing may have changed."

Jim nodded, returned to work. Deliberately he forced himself to forget the passage of time. Carefully he scanned one plate after another, the frown clearing from his forehead as he did so, a half audible hiss of satisfaction escaping from his lips. Daphne glanced at him, but said nothing. She continued with her casual scanning of the plates.

From the end of the hall the young Venusian approached them. Deliberately he picked up the thin metal plates, took one from Daphne's hands, did the same with the one Jim was perusing.

"What?" said Jim, then swore softly. "Damn! Another hour and I'd have had it," he shrugged. "Come on, Daphne, we may as well go."

He led the way out of the building. Above, the sun had reached its zenith, Melik was nowhere in sight. They walked towards their hut.

"I thought that you couldn't speak Venusian," Daphne said.

"Does it make any difference?" Jim asked despondently.

"It could," Daphne smiled. "How would you like to take as long as you wanted over those plates?"

"Why ask?" snapped Jim impatiently. "If we'd had a camera, any form of recording, I could solve our problem. We haven't. I am morally certain that those plates prove my theory to the limit. I had just grasped the trick of deciphering them." He shrugged. "We may as well forget it."

"I can't," Daphne said calmly. "I have an eidetic memory."

CHAPTER TEN

MORTAL COMBAT

Jim took three long strides before the casual remark registered its full impact. He stopped, gripped her shoulders, almost shook her with excitement.

"Eidetic! You mean that you have a photographic memory?"

"Naturally." She squirmed in his grasp. "Jim! You're hurting me!"

"Sorry," he apologised. Nervously he continued the journey towards their hut. "Why didn't you tell me?"

"You kept your own secrets," she reminded.

"I had my reasons for keeping them," he said seriously. "I still have. I want you to promise that you will never tell anyone that I am able to speak Venusian. Will you do that, Daphne?"

"Of course, Jim," she touched his hand. "You may rely on my silence."

"Good," he smiled at her. "How long have you had eidetic memory?"

"All my life. I used to startle the teachers at school. I'd just look at a thing, then could repeat it exactly later on. When I grew older, father made it his habit to take me with him on his expeditions. He said that I was better than any camera."

"You would be," breathed Jim. "No wonder Masters didn't worry about losing his recording equipment. While you were with him, he had a continual source of perfect reference." He began to quiver with anticipation. "Daphne. Could you draw a facsimile of those records we've just seen?"

"Yes."

"Will you? Draw them I mean? If I could only study them at leisure, I know that I'd be able to read them."

"You don't want me to do it here, do you?"

"No. I'd hate for the old man to know that his precious records were now common property. Somehow I don't think that he'd like it. We must get back to the settlement."

Someone called from the end of the village. At a second call, Jim turned. He halted. Melik came swiftly towards them. Despite his haste, his breathing showed no signs of distress.

"Have you examined the records?"

"We have," Jim answered gravely. "The time allowed was short, but the experience was a memorable one."

"I had intended for it to be repeated," said the old custodian. "Now I fear that cannot be."

"Have we offended?" Jim asked quickly.

"No. But there is grave trouble in the place from whence you came. I feel that your presence there would be of use. Will you go?"

"Certainly." He turned to Daphne. "It seems that there is trouble in the settlement. I have a good idea of what it is, I must go back. You can stay here, next to your father. I'll return when things have quietened down."

"No, Jim." She turned to Melik. "My father is unable to travel. Will you tend him if I return?"

"We will."

"Thank you," Daphne smiled at Jim. "I'm coming with you."

"No."

"Why not, Jim?"

"Because there is danger for you at the settlement. I would prefer you to stay here. There is more at stake than you seem to realise." He tried to put hidden emphasis into his tones.

"I want to come with you," she said simply. There was no more arguing.

The trip back took but part of the time they had originally taken. Their guide, a slender youth, glided between towering trees, clumps of matted fronds, skirted swampy ground, with a calm certainty of his direction. Unhindered by excess clothing, or the necessity of carrying a stretcher, both Terrans made good time, though twice Jim had to motion the native to slow his pace. At the Edge, their guide left them. He stood on the edge of the cleared circle, raised an arm in salute, and abruptly was gone. Jim grinned at Daphne.

"Now for the hard part. We've twenty miles to do before dark, think you can manage it?"

Daphne squared her slim shoulders. "I can try," she looked at the sun, now well past the zenith. Jim noticed the direction of her gaze.

"We'll camp the night," he decided.

"I can make it, Jim," she insisted.

"Maybe, but I doubt if I can," he grinned at her. "We've been travelling since before dawn. I feel all in. I'll make a bower, and we can take turns to watch. Don't argue now," he snapped in mock irritation. "You gather some clean ferns, while I look for fruit."

Rapidly he fashioned a lean-to, sat before it, gnawing at a great golden cluster of grape-like fruits. Daphne sat beside him, her head resting against his arm. Aside from the muted drone of winged insects, the jungle was silent.

"What are you thinking of, Jim?" she asked sleepily.

"Nothing much," he grinned. "Wish we had some wine."

"Drunkard," she laughed, then noticing the expression on his face, sobered. "I'm sorry, Jim. Why do you drink so heavily?"

"Were you in love with Conroy?"

"I get it. No personal questions. I thought I was, Jim. Let's just say that I was mistaken."

Somewhere in the distance a branch snapped. Jim tensed, one hand darting towards the holstered flame pistol. Something went lumbering through the matted ferns; he relaxed.

"This is heavenly," sighed Daphne contentedly. "Why couldn't it always be like this?"

"Because men won't let it," Jim said absently. "They want to improve it, make a world fit for men to live in." He laughed curtly. "Telescreens, airports, the mad rat race of getting money so that you can get more money. Work to eat, and eat so that you are able to work. Civilisation!"

"It's not all bad, Jim," Daphne protested. "Men have done wonderful things. Medicine, communications, space flight. You can't sneer at those achievements."

"The Venusians have medical knowledge equal to ours—your father proves it. They have a system of communications spanning their world. How else did Melik know of the trouble at the settlement? Know that we had killed that reptile? You mention space travel, what good has it done anyone? It does us no good, and it means hell to the peoples we contact." Jim shifted restlessly. "Be proud if you like, Daphne, but don't delude yourself."

"You can't live in an ivory tower, Jim. The world is what it is, not what we'd like it to be. We must accept that, or turn away from it, and live in a world of make-believe. The insane asylums are full of such people. Are you like them?"

"Insane do you mean?" Jim shrugged. "I don't know. I can't say that I really care. All I know is that a great people are in danger, and the blind fools can't see it."

"The Venusians? They do see it, Jim. What of the Watchers?"

"Yes. They have the Watchers, the most hated men in the settlement. Tell me, Daphne. If we were to return to Earth, speak of the wonderful vein of ore, bearing easily fissionable elements that we had discovered, what would happen?"

"But we haven't discovered such a vein."

"But what if we had?"

"Why they'd mine it, refine the element…" Her voice trailed into silence.

"You begin to understand," Jim said bitterly. "What would it matter where that vein was located? It could be in Elerdris itself, but would that stop the miners? They would exterminate anything that stood in their path. They would raze the city. What would a few natives matter?"

"There would be compensation," Daphne said weakly.

"Compensation for what? Decided by whom? These people have no use for interplanetary credits. What could they buy? Guns? Telescreens? Clothes they don't need. Metals they don't want? No. If our two civilisations ever come into really close contact, we would destroy them. It has happened before. The aborigines of Australia, living a primitive life, died when they attempted to ape the ways of the white man. They weren't murdered, the white man tried to help them, but they died all the same. It took a long time for the invaders to realise they just could not help them, that the only thing they could do was to leave them alone. How long will it take us to realise the same thing?"

The sun had almost reached the edge of the visible sky, soon it would be dark. Daphne shivered, pressed closer to Jim.

"You frighten me with your talk," she scolded. "What shift shall I keep?"

"Sorry," he smiled down at her. The dying light threw her wide blue eyes into prominence. Once again he was reminded of the sharp bird-like quality of her features, almost child-like in the openness of her expression, the clearness of her skin still faintly tanned from the sunlight of distant Earth.

His arm slipped around her, drew her close. Tenderly he rested her head against his shoulder, and neither of them spoke.

A twig snapped. A bush rustled, someone laughed, someone else sneered. Jim looked up.

"Hello, Fleetan," he said calmly. "And you too, Conroy. You must have been travelling."

The two men stood staring down at him. The Terran, clothed in his impeccable drill shirt and trousers, the Venusian, wearing the flowing robe, and the blazing ruby of his ring. Conroy held a flame pistol, the squat barrel directed at Jim's legs; he laughed.

"Move, Warren," he invited. "Move, and let me see how far you can get without any legs."

"Jack!" Daphne cried. "What are you doing?"

"Shut up you—" Conroy snarled a word that sent the blood pounding through Jim's temples. Daphne looked at him with startled wonder.

"What did you call me?"

Fleetan stepped forward, laid a restraining hand on Conroy's arm, depressing the flame pistol.

"Wait." He turned to Jim. "We had an agreement you and I. Have you kept it?"

"As well as you have," Jim said calmly. "Did you send that merchant into the jungle?"

"It is no longer important." Fleetan dismissed the dead man with a gesture. "There is a debt between us, I think."

"There is," Jim said grimly. "You should be on Earth, Fleetan. They appreciate the art of treachery there. You would do well. First you try to arouse the half-breeds. You give Conroy a radio, knowing that if he used it, he would die at the hands of the Watchers. Then you sent a man to ambush us on the trail. What did you offer him, Fleetan? The price must have been high, or maybe you threatened him? As you say, it doesn't matter now. He paid the Watchers' penalty."

"As you will, Warren. As you will."

"Will I?" Jim stirred, pushed Daphne away from him. "Where is your pride, Fleetan? A member of the old race, of pure-blooded descent, you have a debt you say. A debt of blood. Do you hire killers to collect your debts of honour?"

The red eyes of the tall Venusian widened, seemed to glow with rage, abruptly he slipped off the robe. The white skin of his flesh rippled with long flat muscles. Clad only in a loin cloth, he stood there, a perfect specimen of a noble savage. He flexed his hands.

"Once you struck me, Warren. To lay hands on one of the pure blood is an insult that can only be wiped out in death. I could choose my weapons, instead I will choose none. I will do to you as you did to me. With naked hands we fight, and I shall tear the living flesh from your bones."

Smoothly Jim flowed to his feet, he stripped off his shirt, stepped behind the bower, returned wearing a twist of cloth about his hips. "I am ready, Fleetan."

"Wait!" Conroy moved forward, the pistol steady in his hand. "You promised him to me, Fleetan."

"If he should succeed, or if you think that he may win this combat, then shoot," Fleetan smiled grimly. "And, Conroy, do not kill with the first shot."

"No," said the Terran thickly. "First the legs, then each arm, finally, when he pleads for death, the head."

"What's the matter with you, Conroy?" Daphne half screamed. "You're acting like a beast, like a madman. What has Jim ever done to you that you should hate him so?"

"Don't you know?" Conroy sneered.

"Jim," Daphne said desperately. "You must not fight. Look at you, bruised all over. You wouldn't have a chance."

"Stay out of this," snapped Jim. He flexed his hands, wincing as the bruised muscles of shoulders and body sent stabs of pain through him.

Daphne stared at them, eyes wide and strangely glittering. Suddenly she dived for the discarded weapon belt. Conroy snapped up his pistol, finger white around the trigger. Jim stepped forward, kicked, and the flame pistol went skittering across the loam, inches from Daphne's outstretched hand.

"Leave it," ordered Jim sharply.

"But…."

"Leave it!" He turned to the waiting Venusian. "One thing, Fleetan."

"Yes?"

"Your quarrel is with me. The girl is harmless. Have I your word that she shall be unharmed?"

"If you win, she shall not be harmed," replied the native evasively.

"And if I lose?"

Fleetan shrugged, glanced at Conroy, and suddenly lunged forward hands outstretched.

Jim was almost taken unawares. He had automatically followed the movement of Fleetan's eyes. Just in time he jerked his attention back to the Venusian.

He sidestepped, swung a hard right to the head, grunted as pain shot up his cracked knuckles. The Venusian snarled, crouched, suddenly kicked viciously. Jim stepped back, grabbed at the foot, missed, bored in, both hands working.

He knew that he had to end this combat quickly. He hadn't the stamina for a prolonged battle. He must end it quickly and then tackle Conroy. Within him, a dull ache rose at the thought of what would happen to Daphne should he fail.

He felt the impact of his fists on the native's hard torso, dodged a wild grab, weaved closer pounding at the marble whiteness of the muscled flesh. He wondered a little why Fleetan, a man unused to fighting with his fists, should have chosen personal combat. It was the only favourable thing about the whole business.

A knee lunged at him; Jim twisted, letting the blow strike his thigh, he grabbed at a wrist, twisted, jerked and felt his foot slip on the soft dirt.

Desperately he tried to regain his balance. Fleetan, sensing his opportunity, thrust his weight against him. Together they fell, writhing in the top layer of rotting ferns.

Jim jerked his head aside as stiffened fingers stabbed at his eyes. The long nails raked his forehead, sending blood rilling into his eyes. He clenched his hand, smashed at the delicate nose feeling the bone yield beneath the hammering blow. Fleetan screamed, then Jim felt the full strength of the man.

It was incredible! Muscles rippled like wire ropes. He concentrated on saving his eyes. Fleetan stabbed at them again and again, smashed his stiffened palm across the1 bridge of Jim's nose, pounded his mouth. Pain flooded the Terran as the broken bone of his nose sent fresh waves of agony through his head. He snarled, rage sending a gush of adrenaline flowing through his body. He twisted, beat aside, hands, arms, elbows, found the thick muscled throat.

Desperately he drove his thumbs deep into the Venusian's windpipe. Jim knew it was his last chance; gritting his teeth, bending his head to avoid the frantic blows of the writhing native, he concentrated on squeezing his hands together. Dimly he felt something yield. Dimly he realised that Fleetan no longer showered him with blows. The struggles of the native weakened, died.

Still Jim drove iron fingers into the now soft throat.

Slowly the mad rage left him. Slowly sense returned. He released his grip, lurched to his feet, took a stumbling stride forward.

Conroy lifted the squat barrel of the flame pistol.

CHAPTER ELEVEN

DANGER

Jim stared dully at the pitted orifice of the weapon. He felt curiously detached, light-headed. The dying light threw the flame pistol into sharp relief. The flared muzzle, the cooling vanes leading back to the swelling curve of the firing chamber, the ringed butt. A golden gleam came from beneath the trigger guard, the gleam of Conroy's signet ring. Jim looked at it, and stood there, waiting.

Conroy laughed without humour.

"Is he dead?"

Jim didn't answer. Conroy moved closer, gesturing with the pistol. "I said, is he dead?"

"I don't know." Jim spoke painfully. He wiped blood from his eyes, tore his gaze away from the menacing weapon.

"I hope he is," said Conroy. "I hope his soul rots in hell." He licked his lips. "I'm going to kill you, Warren. I'm going to kill you and then I'll attend to the girl."

His laughter echoed eerily through the silent jungle. "Why don't you beg, Warren? Why don't you plead with me to spare you, and save the girl?"

Jim stood silent, staring at the insane flecks of light glowing in Conroy's eyes.

Something about his calm impassivity infuriated the Terran, he stepped forward, raising the pistol.

"Swine!" he spat. "Robbing swine!" he swung the gun in a vicious arc.

Jim ducked, the heavy barrel scraping the top of his head, he slammed his fist into Conroy's stomach, jerked upwards with his knee. Conroy screamed, fell to the dirt, the pistol flying from his fingers. Swiftly Jim scooped it from the loam.

"Daphne," he called. "Daphne!"

She didn't answer. Carefully keeping watch on the groaning Terran, Jim let his gaze flicker over the camp. A huddled figure caught his eye, he dropped to his knees beside her.

"Daphne! Wake up, Daphne!"

He shook her, slapped her face, slowly she responded.

"Jim! I thought that you were dead!" She held her hand to her temple. A dark bruise marred the smooth flesh. "Conroy hit me with the flame pistol," she explained. "Knocked me out." Her eyes widened as she saw the groaning man. "Are you all right, Jim? What happened?"

"I think Fleetan's dead," Jim said rapidly. "Conroy grew careless, came too close. He'll be all right." He helped her to her feet. "How about yourself?"

"I'll make out," she smiled tremulously. "A bit of a headache, but that's all. What shall we do, Jim?"

"You'll see." He handed her his own pistol. "Keep watch, they may have friends nearby."

Conroy still writhed on the soft loam, hands clutched to his middle. Jim turned him over with the toe of his boot, gestured with the pistol.

"Get up, Conroy. It didn't hurt that much."

"What do you want?"

"Get up!" Jim thrust with his boot.

Slowly Conroy climbed to his feet. He looked ill, the sweat standing in globules on face and neck. He licked thin lips.

"You came here," snapped Jim. "How?"

"We came in Fleetan's private helicopter."

"Where is it?"

"Not far, about half a mile," Conroy sounded sullen. "We didn't want to warn you."

"Naturally," Jim said ironically. "How did you know that we would be here?"

"I didn't. Fleetan did; he said that you and Daphne had been together several days, and that she was in love with you."

"So you tried to kill me," Jim shrugged. "Now it's your turn."

"What do you mean?" Conroy swallowed, tried to still the quivering of his hands. "I wouldn't have killed you. I only wanted to hurt you a little, get my own back for what you did to me. You can't kill me, Warren. I'm Terran, the same as you are. You daren't kill me."

"How sure are you of that?" Jim asked quietly. The gun jerked in his hand. "Where's the plane?"

"I'll guide you," stammered Conroy. "I'll show you where it is, but don't kill me, Warren. Don't kill me!"

Jim grunted disgustedly, bent to examine the lax body of the native. Fleetan was dead. Jim stared at him for long moment.

"Let's get going."

They moved in silence towards the helicopter.

It was dark when they landed. Jim set the plane down just outside the limits of the settlement, turned to the others.

"I'll leave you here. Conroy can pilot the helicopter into the Terran area. You'll be safe there."

"Where are you going, Jim?" Daphne asked. She leaned forward anxiously, the dim lights from the instrument panel illuminating her face.

"I can't enter the area," explained Jim. "I'll be at the House of Welcome if you want to contact me. You can inform the Port Commander of Conroy's attempt to kill you, if you wish. Personally, I'd prefer that he caught the next ship home."

"I'll do that," promised Conroy eagerly. "I must have been mad. I know that this sounds strange, Warren, but I'm sorry for what I did. Can you believe that?"

"I think I can," Jim said. "In any case, best to forge the whole thing." He opened the panel. "Incidentally Conroy, here is your flame pistol. Would you mind checking the loading?"

Conroy stared at him, then opened the gun. The chamber was empty!

"I haven't touched it," Jim said. He stepped back, watched while the vanes whirled, watched until the flying lights had vanished above the trees, shrugged, strode towards the sprawling buildings of the settlement.

Men stood tensely about the streets. They idled in the narrow alleys, lingered in doorways, sat in little groups in the wine shops. Sullen-looking men. Young, with white skin and dark, vari-coloured hair. Half-breeds.

They stared with brooding eyes. Their fingers twitched restlessly, fingering imaginary weapons. Faces were hard, grim-looking, lined with irritation. The direction of their gaze was the same, the glaring lights of the fenced Terran area.

Jim touched one on the shoulder, stepped back as the man whirled with a startled curse.

"Where can I find Pheelan?"

"Who are you?" snapped the man. "What does a Terran want with Pheelan?"

"My name is Warren," Tim said coldly. "Where is Pheelan?"

"You are a Terran." The man spat contemptuously. "Find him yourself." He turned away.

Jim gripped his shoulder, spun him around, glared into the young features. "Where is Pheelan?" he snapped. "Tell me or I'll kill you." The knife he had taken from the spaceman snapped open in his fist. He let the light gleam on the blade, jerked it forward until the point dug into flesh.

"Tell me!"

The half-breed licked his lips, stared nervously about him. He was alone, one of the reasons Jim approached him.

"I do not know."

"You lie! Tell me where to find Pheelan, or I'll—"

"In the wine shop of Sal Cleenar," gasped the man. He reeled beneath Jim's sudden push. "The curse of the Watchers upon you," he shrieked as Jim strode away "Terran dog! Your hour is near."

Jim ignored the frenzied shouting. Diving down narrow alleys, skirting the brighter lights, and the more heavily frequented spots, he moved quickly across the settlement towards the edge of the built area. As he passed near the high wire-mesh fence, he could see alerted guards, the Wilson guns ready in capable hands, pacing behind the closed barrier. Others, high on watch towers, swung the slender barrels of semi-portables in menacing arcs. The entire area and immediate surrounds, blazed with light.

The market was deserted, the merchants gone. No Terrans were in the streets, and Jim saw only native Venusians and half-breeds. The air was heavy with tension.

He was gasping when he came in sight of the low doored wine shop. His side hurt and the cut on his temple had opened. He trembled, his hands jerking, his muscles quivering uncontrollably. In the stained and torn shirt and trousers, he made a wild picture. Several men move forward purposely as he entered the pool of soft light thrown from the open doorway.

"Stay where you are, Terran."

"My name is Warren. I must talk with Pheelan," Jim gasped. "Is he here?"

"Warren?" the man frowned. "Warren is in Eledris. How can you be, Warren?"

"I am Warren. I returned an hour ago. Where is Pheelan?"

"I know Warren." One of the other guards pushed himself forward, peered at the gasping Terran. "This is he."

"Thanks," panted Jim. He entered the low door of the wine shop.

It was thronged with men, all of them of dual parentage. Great containers of wine stood about on the low tables, the sweet, slightly sickly smell of the thick green liquid, heavy on the close air. Jim licked parched lips, seized a cup from the hand of a man near him, drained it at a draught.

"More," he croaked.

Wine slopped over his hand, greedily he drank and the wine quelled his thirst, cleared his head, steadied his senses. He set down the cup.

"Where is Pheelan?"

He came thrusting through the crowd, the scarred face expressing his wonder at seeing his visitor. "Jim! I didn't expect you."

"So I notice," Jim said grimly. He looked about him. "What's this? The gathering of your forces?"

"No, Jim." Pheelan led him to a table, dismissed the others with a curt gesture. "Sit down. You look half dead. What has happened?"

"Plenty. It can wait, I'll tell you later." He tried to still the quivering of his hands, the trembling of his muscles. "What has happened?"

"Trouble. A Terran was killed yesterday. The redheaded spaceman you had trouble with, remember? The rest of them have stayed behind the wire since then. Naturally we got the blame."

"He probably asked for it," Jim grunted. "But I thought that your people had better sense."

"It wasn't our fault, Jim!" Pheelan leaned forward earnestly. "I know that some of us are weak but we are still few enough for me to know every half-breed on this planet. I've questioned them all. None admit to having killed that Terran."

"One of them could be lying."

"No. I know them too well. If one of them had done it, I should know."

"You seem very sure of yourself?"

"I am," Pheelan nodded emphatically. "Believe me, Jim. None of us killed that Terran."

"You know what you are saying?" Jim snapped. "He wouldn't have died at the hands of his own kind. You are telling me that he was killed by a native. Why?"

Pheelan shrugged. "Who knows? A quarrel over a woman perhaps. An angry merchant. Any of a dozen reasons. He was not a likeable man."

"How did he die?"

"A needle gun, the darts hit him in the face."

"I see," Jim nodded, reached for the wine container. "So his death has set off this trouble. I suppose the men are eager to get hold of those Wilson guns, and start a war. What does his death mean to them?"

"Before they locked themselves behind the wire, they avenged the death of their comrade. Twenty men of the garrison rioted in Dile Nalleth's wine shop. They wrecked the place. Three half-breeds were murdered. Dile Nalleth's widow will bear a fatherless son."

"Now I understand." Jim breathed deeply, winced a the pain in his chest. "Who wanted to start a riot Pheelan? Who was it who gave you the Wilson guns, egged on the wild talk of a war of extermination? The original plan is unworkable now, you cannot take the Terrans by surprise. Who is advising you now?"

"No one is advising me. I am against this stupidity as you well know." Pheelan controlled his anger. "As for the Wilson guns, Fleetan provided them. I discovered that it was he who had bribed the agitator. Why do you ask?"

"The original plan failed. Yet Fleetan still had to create turmoil, quell it, and remain as chief intermediary between Earth and Venus. How better than by killing a Terran, putting the blame onto the half-breeds? The Terrans would avenge themselves. You would be resentful and strike back. A short war of attrition. Fleetan would be master of the situation. Earth would be satisfied, and the half-breeds would no longer be a problem." Jim laughed bitterly. "He must have studied well, while on Earth. Such concepts are strange to the natives. It took the guile of centuries of warfare to learn how to manage such a manoeuvre, to use the cunning of the beast to find a useful scapegoat."

"It could be," mused Pheelan. "I can see how such a thing would work. But, Jim, what does Fleetan hope gain by all this? He is high on the council, beloved of the Watchers, respected by the Elders. What has he to gain!

"Power," Jim said shortly. "Power over the lives men. Power to degrade them, thinking while he does so that he is raising himself. It is a particularly Terran concept, this lusting after power. They cannot find contentment with what they have, they must always be greedy for what their neighbour possesses. It is a thing that has raised them to the heights, but it is a thing which makes mock of all their achievements. They have grown up with the concept. To them it is a part of life, ingrained deep in their civilisation. In *their* civilisation, Pheelan, not yours. A Venusian cannot associate with Terrans, and long retain his sanity. The two cultures are too different."

He reached for the wine.

"It is a fact that Venusians and Terrans cannot mix. Close contact does not harm the Terrans. They are immune to the mental troubles resulting from it. Their way of life is too competitive for it to worry them. They take what they can get, and to the devil with those too weak to stop them. It has hardened them, this perpetual conflict. It has won them the stars."

He drank, looking into the reflection of the lamps shining deep in the thick green wine.

"Fleetan studied on Earth. Despite himself, despite any resolutions he may have made, he became contaminated. He looked about him, and saw what wealth meant to the Terrans. You cannot realise what it does mean, Pheelan. Wealth can buy anything on Earth. Anything. All else pales in comparison with it. Fleetan wanted wealth. He wanted to enjoy it. To do that he had to reside on Earth. His plan was simple, but he did his best. Murder the half-breeds, pander to the Terran forces, obtain the office which would keep him in wealth and power.

He would have spoilt his own world to do it. Seen the jungles ravished for minerals, the natives exploited for labour, the villages turned into tourist camps. The result was inevitable."

"Yes?"

"Fleetan went mad. His mind cracked beneath the pull of opposing loyalties. In the end, even his judgment yielded to bestial lust of combat."

"How do you know these things?"

"I met Fleetan," Jim smiled. "He is dead."

Pheelan leaped to his feet with a savage roar.

CHAPTER TWELVE

DISCOVERY

At the sound, men stilled their murmured conversation. Wine cups clinked as they were set on the tables. Within seconds a crowd had gathered around them.

Pheelan stood, legs wide, eyes blazing, the scar standing out like a scarlet gash against the whiteness of his cheek. "Dead?" he bellowed. "Fleetan dead?"

"Dead," repeated Jim. He stared at the assembled men. "Get back to your places. This conversation is private."

"Never mind that." A man thrust himself forward. "What's this about, Fleetan?"

"He's dead."

"Dead? Who killed him Did you?"

"No. I tried, but I wasn't strong enough. I didn't kill Fleetan, much as he deserved it."

"Then who did? Was it the Terrans?"

"No."

"Then who?"

"The Watchers," said Jim calmly, and smiled at their instinctive recoiling from the table.

"The Watchers!" The whisper ran around the low room. Men glanced furtively at them, backed away. Within seconds again the arena around the table was clear. Jim looked at Pheelan.

"Well?"

"I'm not sorry," grunted the half-breed. "He caused enough trouble. What happened?"

Jim told him. "I thought that I had over-estimated his strength. I was desperate, but even then I was too weak to win. I felt him go limp, his muscles relaxing. It wasn't until I examined him, discovered the dart, that I knew why. Someone had shot him from the edge of the jungle. Who else but a Watcher?"

"But why should they, Jim?" Pheelan frowned. "They should have killed you. You were the alien; Fleetan was a true blooded native. Why should the Watchers protect you?"

"I've wondered about that," admitted Jim. "I don't know. They did, and I'm thankful to them for it."

"Well," said Pheelan. "That ends the trouble anyway. Without Fleetan to promise supplies of Wilson guns and ammunition, we can forget all thoughts of extermination."

"Are you sorry?"

"No. It was the wrong way." He sighed, reached for the wine. "Did you have any success?"

"Yes. Melik allowed me and the girl to examine the records. We didn't have long, but I know that they hold the answer."

"You mean that you can prove our common origin?"

"Yes."

"What are you going to do about it?"

"Publish the news of course. Press for legislature to allow for free travel, equal rights. With the evidence I have, it should be a simple matter."

"But you have no proof. No records."

"I shall get them," promised Jim.

Pheelan looked down at his wine, his fingers curling around the cup. "You realise what this will mean of course," he asked quietly. "Earth will regard Venus as a poor relation. They will feel a moral right to bring us the benefits of their civilisation. It will be the mental death to all we hold sacred."

"*We* hold sacred, Pheelan?" Jim looked at the half-breed, eyes narrowed in sudden suspicion. "Tell me, how are you so sure that none of the half-breeds killed that Terran?"

"I am sure," insisted the man stubbornly.

"The Watchers would be sure," Jim murmured softly. "They would know, they know everything. Are you a Watcher, Pheelan?"

"Are you mad? The Watchers killed my mother."

"So you told me, yet you could be a Watcher, Pheelan. Your hair could be dyed, your cheek scarred, you could be wearing contact lenses to disguise the colour of your eyes. Are you a Watcher?"

"What's the matter with you, Jim? You know that I'm not a Watcher."

"They killed my father," breathed Jim. "Even on Earth he wasn't safe from them. They killed him." The blade of his knife snapped open, the light gleaming from the razor sharp steel. "Are you a Watcher?"

"You must be drunk!" Pheelan looked about him uneasily. "If any of the others should hear you, my life wouldn't be worth a dead leaf. Stop talking nonsense."

"Is it nonsense?" Jim breathed thickly, his eyes dull and glazed looking. "They killed my father. When I was a child they killed him. I loved my father, he taught me Venusian. You know Venusian don't you, Pheelan? How did you learn it? Your mother died when you were born you told me. If you can speak it, then why not the other half-breeds? Shall I ask them?"

The prick of the dart was just one more pain among many. For a moment Jim sat staring at the tiny sliver of wood, his mind struggling to realise just what it meant. He felt numb, light-headed, incapable of movement or sound. Through the dimness of his vision he saw Pheelan staring at him, saw the tiny orifice of the needle gun.

"I'm sorry, Jim," Pheelan said.

As blackness roared down upon him, Jim realised that the half-breed had meant exactly what he said. He tried to grin, failed, felt the knife falling from his slack fingers.

He never felt the edge of the table as he hit it on his way to the floor.

* * * *

From a great distance he heard voices, saw a dull gleam of hazy light, felt a cold impact as something wet and cold struck his face. He coughed, blinked his eyes, sat upright.

He was in a low-roofed hut, the floor was of tamped dirt, the furnishings poor and broken. With a mild shock of surprise he recognised it as his own.

Light flowed from the primitive lamp. A man moved, smiled down at him.

"Hello, Jim. Feel better?"

Jim swallowed, tried to rid his body of the numbing effect of alien drugs. "What do you think?" he muttered. At the second attempt he managed to stand up, stumbled to one of the shaky chairs, slumped into it.

Pheelan touched his wrist, peeled back the lid of one eye, nodded. "You'll be out of it soon, Jim. Here, have a drink." He thrust a goblet of wine across the table.

Jim drank, the wine rilling over his chin, wiping his face he peered at the Venusian. "So I was right. You are a Watcher!"

"Yes."

"You did it well," Jim said bitterly. "Who would suspect a half-breed? From the settlement you could watch everything that went on, report frequently. Why did you do it, Pheelan? Why?"

"Because of what I believe in," Pheelan said quietly. "I am a half-breed, Jim. My father was a Terran; that was no disguise. You were wrong there."

"But...?" Jim broke off as a man stepped from the shadows.

"Perhaps I had better explain, Warren." Melik drew up a chair, the light shining from his snow-white hair, his skin the colour of fresh milk. The old custodian rested his arms on the table, stared at Jim with his wide ruby eyes. "Don't look so surprised. I am a Watcher, many of us are. We hope that you will be one also."

"Join with those who killed my father?" Jim pursed his lips as if he tasted something foul. "Never."

"We did not kill your father, Warren. We have killed none except those who ignored our warnings. We are not murderers. We are men devoted to a cause Will you hear me?"

"Have I a choice?"

"Yes. You may leave this place now, and none will harm you. Well?"

"What have you to say?"

Melik sighed, letting his thin lids droop over suddenly tired eyes. "It is a long story, Warren, but try to be patient and understand. The Watchers are a legend. The Watchers who kill, who rule, who terrorise, exist only in the minds of the credulous and the uninformed. It was legend fostered deliberately, for a purpose, for one single object. So far it has worked."

Delicately he poured wine, letting a thin stream of the green liquid fall from a height into a goblet of yellow glass. He sipped slowly, swallowed, set down the goblet.

"Venus isn't Earth, Warren. Twenty thousand of your years ago our forebears came here, came here from Earth. Your theory is perfectly correct. We are of one common root. Why they came, why they stayed, is to be found the records. It does not concern us now, but on Venus grew a new civilisation, a civilisation devoted not to mechanical progress, but to mental. Not the external, but the internal."

"So I was right!"

"Yes, but allow me to continue. Our forebears turned their backs on all their mechanical knowledge. Machines rusted to dust. Books mouldered. All became as nothing. The records they kept, we have them yet. Of the rest, there remains nothing." Melik paused, stared through time to the distant past.

"The conquest of the mind began. To live a simple primitive life, to rid ourselves of the lust for gain, the innate cruelty of the beast, the insane desire for power. To re-fashion what we were, into what we hoped to become. It was not easy. Slowly we began to alter our values. Slowly we grew aware of the tremendous power of the mind. Steadily we progressed, year after year, generation after generation, until the Terrans came— and the progress of twenty thousand years was at stake."

"Didn't that prove the slowness of your progress?"

"No. We watched the Terrans, what they were, how they acted, and we knew that we had been right. The old stock hadn't changed, but we had. Yet even after twenty thousand years we had not changed enough. Contact would destroy us. Black is stronger than white. A particle of black, no matter how small, will turn what is white into something less than that. Our civilisation was imperilled."

"So you founded the Watchers?" Jim mused.

"We invented the Watchers," corrected the old man.

"Some few of us volunteered to contact the Terrans. Brave men and women who sacrificed themselves for the good of the whole. In some degree they managed to influence the invaders, quell a little of the restless spirit inherent within them, confine them to one small area. The rest of us withdrew."

"You can't lessen reality by ignoring it."

"We knew that. We didn't ignore it, but we had to isolate it. The legend of the Watchers grew. Fostered by the original Venusians, inflated by the Terrans, believed in by the offspring of dual parentage. Atrocity stories, tales of swift vengeance, the insistence on omnipotent knowledge. The Watchers served as a wall between the invaders and ourselves."

"True stories!" snapped Jim. "You killed my father!"

"No. He died, that is true, but he died from an Earthly disease, hastened by the death of your mother. We do not kill, we have no need for that. Have you ever heard of the Anero Tanap?"

"The hidden place?"

"No. Not the hidden place, the unknown place. The mind, Warren. The mind! Now do you understand?"

"Amnesia!" Jim jerked upright in his chair. "Of course, the hypnotic conviction. The mother forgets her child, the child is convinced that his mother died," he laughed quietly. "Simple when you know how."

"It took twenty thousand years to learn mind control," Melik reminded. "Mind control, and other things. We do have Watchers in the jungle, a few men, very few, who patrol the paths, and follow expeditions. One such found the man sent by Fleetan; he had to die. Fleetan also, his mind had broken, and he would have killed you. The Terran, we did not worry about, he had unloaded his pistol, believing that he was loading it."

"I see," Jim stared at his wine. "I suspected something like that. A dozen little things, but all adding to an unbelievable total. That is why I guessed Pheelan was a Watcher. I did not expect that he would prove it so well."

"The dart was an anaesthetic, we could not have you betraying your suspicions. Men like Pheelan are hard to find."

"I can imagine they would be," grinned Jim. He swallowed his wine. "Why are you telling me all this?"

"Because we want you to become one of us, Warren. We want you to become a Watcher."

"But why? To prevent a few Terrans entering your jungles? To keep an eye on things in general? What is the whole point of your seclusion? You can't hide yourselves forever."

"We don't intend to," Melik lifted his thin lids, the ruby eyes blazing with inner power. "We are at a crisis, Warren. The experiment of twenty thousand years is at its climax. Now more than ever we must be left alone. You know what happens when Terran and Venusian meet. There is conflict. The language, the mental approach, the very style of cultures are mutually opposing. We cannot yet meet the challenge. They have come too soon."

"What can I do, persuade them to go home? You know that's impossible. When I publish my findings they will pour into Venus, how can anyone stop them?"

"You must not publish your findings."

"What?"

"You must keep your knowledge secret. It is essential."

"But why? You let me examine the records. Why did you do that if I must not help the half-breeds with my discoveries?"

"When first you asked to see the records, a long time ago now, you were refused. You wanted to prove you theory for personal gratification. Fame was what you wanted, the results didn't interest you. You know what happened."

"I know," Jim said grimly.

"When next you tried, you had altered. Now it was for the benefit of others that you wanted to justify your theory. That and for one other reason."

"Yes?"

"It was essential for your mental health that you examine them. The desire to prove or disprove your contention had become an obsession with you. Now you are free of that desire. Now you know. You must not use that knowledge."

"So it was mental therapy?" Jim said bitterly. "Pity!"

"Is there anything wrong with pity?"

"No, but all that—for nothing!"

"Knowledge is never wasted," Melik said gently. "Knowing what you know will help you to help us."

"But why?"

"We need one more generation free from interference. One more generation to stabilise the mental power so painfully acquired. We rely on you, and on men like you to give us that time."

"Is it worth it?"

Melik stared at the container of wine. He didn't move, nothing about him moved—but the container lifted into the air, swung, settled down again. Jim sighed.

"Telekinesis."

"Yes. Teleportation, telepathy, group consciousness, all are just within our grasp. Now do you understand?"

"Yes."

"You will never be able to acquire these powers. Nor your children, but one day we shall be able to teach all Terrans, all peoples, and war will be a thing of the past. Is that not worth guarding?"

"Yes." Jim stood up, looked down at the wine, pushed it away with an expression of distaste. "When shall I start?"

"Now."

"No tests?" Jim smiled wryly.

"You have had your tests," Melik smiled. "You will find the girl waiting for you at the House of Welcome. She is a good girl, a fit companion for such as you have become."

"But how can I ask her to marry me?"

"Why not?" Melik smiled. "I knew your father, Jim. A good man, you need not be ashamed of your forebears." He stood by the open door, still smiling, then abruptly he was gone.

Jim sighed, grinned at Pheelan, strode into the night. He thought of Daphne, of the knowledge locked with her memory, and he lengthened his stride. He thought his father, and smiled. Terrans weren't the only ones able to father dual parentage children, Venusians could,d too.

Jim wondered if Daphne would object to marrying a man who'd had a Venusian father, a half-breed.

Somehow, he knew she wouldn't.

www.ingramcontent.com/pod-product-compliance
Lightning Source LLC
Chambersburg PA
CBHW020151180626
46810CB00004B/1843